Sasenarine Persaud

# DEAR DEATH

Peepal Tree Press

First published in Great Britain in 1989
Peepal Tree Press
53, Grove Farm Crescent
Leeds LS16 6BZ
Yorkshire
England

ISBN 0 94883 28 9

For the women and men who have persevered

in 150 years in the west,

Kumar, Jadoo, Shiv, Dhanwanttie and Leslie M.

# *Prologue*

He was tempted to believe that there was something called a soul. Some indefinable spirit which was responsible for consciousness. He was tempted to believe, too, that this soul never died. He liked the explanation that, just as the body wore new clothes, so the soul inhabited new bodies from time to time. It seemed logical that this soul should be able to recall remnants of a past life. Environmentalist theories were frequently shown to be very limited. There were, for instance, brothers exposed to similar home and school situations yet becoming characters inexplicably different. How could you explain how someone, never exposed to painting, started to paint virtually overnight, and paint exceptionally well? True, you could speak of latent talent, but how was this latent talent acquired? Nothing except the phenomenon of the soul, of reincarnation, adequately explained all of this. What of those experiments when people under hypnosis had recounted in vivid detail the experiences of individuals from the historical past? There was verification that these people had not read anything which could account for the stories they told, yet when they where checked by historians, the details were found to be uncannily true.

Then there was the *Gita*; Krishna had told Arjuna on the battlefield that they had both been born before and had met before and that the soul never died. And this came from the holiest book on earth – at least for Hindus, part of the oldest scriptures in the whole world in which the concept of the soul and reincarnation was constantly reiterated. On the other hand, the Bible spoke of the soul and its eternal damnation or salvation. Yet did not the Christians believe that Christ would come again? If that was not reincarnation, what was?

If he were to question the concept of reincarnation how would he go about it – logically? How was it that *he* could not remember his previous life or lives? Then he remembered what Krishna had told Arjuna: that only a person who 'realised' himself was able to recall his previous lives and very few persons were able to do this because very few persons looked into themselves hard enough, and consistently enough. That was the Scripture. But who wrote this scripture and all other scriptures? Men, just like himself. Men who were liable to error and folly, men who were subject to the distortion of their feelings just like himself. Why should he believe unquestioningly in any scripture, any book written by another man? Believers argued that the writers of these scriptures were inspired. This assumed there was a God, and that these scriptures were revealed to these writers, but how could he know that this was so except by taking the word of the writer, a man like himself. If *he* claimed he spoke with God, nobody could prove that that was not so. Yet if he *had* spoken to God, how could he prove it?

Perhaps none of this led anywhere. But what was undeniably true was that he could not remember anything about a previous life or lives. The truth was, as Krishna had said, that he had not 'realised' himself in any sense. He had never thought about it in that way. He had been born some twenty-four years ago. Could he remember his birth? Could he remember anything of the first or second or third or fourth year of his life? That had shaken him. That was the first time he realised he could remember nothing of the first year, nor second year, nor third year nor fourth year of his life. Only twenty years ago. So what chance was there of knowing about a life fifty years ago, never mind a life one hundred and fifty years before that?

# Chapter One

The house was well back in the yard. The fence was very high and he could see through it. There was no green in the fore-yard. It appeared as though the front-yard was ploughed. That was all he could remember and it came in a flash as in the flash of a camera-flick. That was his first, his earliest recollection. He had spoken to his father some years ago and his father had confirmed that description. Dalip had been about five years old and they were living in Alexander Village. What had happened to the first four years of his life? How many times he tried to recollect. Nothing. Nothing came. He had found out where they were living in those four years. He knew the 'history' but that meant nothing.

Even when he recalled the first event in his life that he was conscious of, it was not this event which triggered his memory but one about two years later. He was about six. His mother was going to a place called Berbice. For what, he did not know. This place was far away. It would take almost a whole day to get there. They would spend a week with some relatives. Either he or his brother, a year younger, would accompany his mother. They would have to travel by train. He was excited, hoping that he would be chosen. Though he did not know why, he knew his elder brother could not go and he was glad. He had sensed that his mother wanted him to go. He knew she liked him very much and his younger brother was not as well-behaved as he was; he was very mischievous. His father would want his younger brother, Romesh, to go, but he knew his mother would have the final say. Even so, he was still afraid that Romesh might do something. He was just as keen on making journeys. Both of them used to get away when their mother and father were at work and go to the train station two blocks away, though this was forbidden. They loved to look at the trains though they were afraid of these green giants that seemed always to come straight at them and make a terrible noise. They admired the people who travelled in the trains which went to the end of the world. The trains always got smaller and smaller and disappeared. They too longed to travel on these trains to the end of the world and the end of the line. Here was the chance. Somehow, Romesh had realised that he would not be the one to accompany his mother. He became more insistent out of spite. There was always intense rivalry between them. They always fought to outdo each other. This was helped along because their mother always seemed to like Dalip, and their father, Romesh. At no time, it appeared, could their parents afford to buy two sets of things for them. One always got at one time and the other some other time. It had seemed to Dalip that it was because of this that he was given the pair of new shoes bought about two months before and Romesh the pair of new socks.

It was finally settled the evening before that Dalip would accompany his mother. He was happy as he helped his mother pack. Romesh was nowhere around. Dalip was too happy to notice where Romesh was.

Their father had not only agreed that Dalip would go to Berbice but he had also added that Dalip would use Romesh's new socks since, if it had been the other way round, Romesh would have used Dalip's new shoes. Dalip was glad to hear this. It had been one of the rare occasions his father ruled in his favour. He was glad also because he felt that he should have new things for the trip. However, he was most happy because, when the shoes and socks had been bought, he had wanted both for himself. He had felt that he should have gotten both because he always behaved better than Romesh and he always did better than Romesh at school. To get them both for the trip was no more than he deserved.

On the morning of the journey they woke up very early. It was very dark outside. Everything was prepared and was in readiness. His mother was dressed and ready but she was with his father in the bedroom. All that Dalip still had to do was to put on his socks and shoes. He had put his shoes with the socks in them under the cabinet the night before. He stretched his hand and pulled out the shoes but there were no socks. He knew immediately that Romesh had hidden them. He wanted to cry. He did not know what to do. His mother and father came out of the bedroom and saw him motionless. When his father realised what had happened he seized Romesh asking him where he had hidden the socks. Romesh did not answer. His father asked again and again, more threateningly each time. Romesh refused to answer. The trains seemed to whistle. His father boxed Romesh's ears. Dalip wanted to shout that they would miss the train. His father released Romesh. His mother returned with Dalip's old socks.

They were out in the half light, his father with the bags. To the station, into the train. And it was moving.

Dalip was calm and happy. His dream of travelling in a train was becoming a reality. He was happy that he was alone with his mother. He always had to share her with his elder brother and his younger brother and his father. She placed him facing her and he liked that; he could do two things. He could see all the strange exciting places they passed through, and he could see his mother. He would do his best to remember everything as he saw it. Almost fifteen years later, when he revisited the places they were almost exactly as he remembered.

After the first mile or so the train seemed to sing and Dalip had loved it. He saw the birds outside. He could hear them above the sound of the train which sometimes seemed to travel so close to the trees that he felt he could have stretched out and touched them. He saw birds on some of the trees. He saw cars like ants on a road that seemed every now and then to be close to the train. The train crossed two bridges which seemed very close to the black water. He was scared. The bridges seemed so narrow and he had wondered how such small bridges could hold such a long train. He was glad when the train reached the other bank. During this time he hardly looked at his mother. He had glanced at her when they were on the bridges and she seemed to be looking intently outside. The moment he had seen the direction of her gaze he remembered what he was missing outside and he forgot her. However, when she gave him food from one of the bags, he scarcely took his eyes off her though he quickly looked outside when she looked at him.

The train stopped at a station. It seemed to Dalip that they had been travelling for a long while. He could not be sure. He hardly bothered about time. But they could not have reached their destination because he had got the idea from his elder brother, who had made the trip already, that they had to cross a particularly wide river. So far they had crossed only small streams. But the train stopped and they got off the train with their bags. They went into a station which seemed to have smooth marble flooring. The floor seemed glazed and the light from the fluorescent tubes made it shine even more. The place had a peculiar smell. The shine and the smell made Dalip think of a hospital, but he couldn't be sure whether this was part of the original memory. Then they went into a large room with chairs and sliding windows just like those in the train. Dalip was convinced that this was another train, a larger train. Then his mother took him outside. He gasped. There was water all around. They were high over the water which seemed to be lashing against the train. They went to the edge and he was afraid. He held his mother's fingers tightly and when she stopped at some rails at the edge of the train he clung to her leg. If he looked too intently he would fall down, down into the water. Then he noticed that the train was moving – on water. He was puzzled. Trains did not move on water and yet he was sure they were on another train. No – they must be on a boat as the thing was moving on water just like his brother had said. Dalip was disappointed. His brother had said the boat was large and very beautiful. He had come onto this beautiful thing without being aware of it, as though it was just another train. But he was afraid. Afraid of the rough water. It took so long to

10

reach the other bank. Could the boat sink? He clung tighter to his mother. Then she started to point and tell him things. He was too scared to hear and later when she stooped close to him he was too happy to see or bother with anything other than her tenderness and her attention. When the boat finally reached the other side they went into another train, but shortly after they disembarked again. It was almost dark. His mother said they had arrived. He was tired.

Dalip hardly saw his mother that week. This strange place was a new world. He hardly spoke to anyone. There was nobody as young as himself. There were grown-ups like his mother and they always seemed to be with his mother, talking. There was, though, a girl, much older than Dalip, who would talk to him and take him for walks. He liked holding her hand and walking through the strange streets she seemed to know. She seemed to like it too. Yet she seemed to be free only during the afternoons. Most of the day he would be left to himself.

The happiest day of that week was the one afternoon when his mother took him for a walk – through what seemed like a little town. She explained things but he hardly took anything in. She bought things which he ate. He did not know what they were, but his mother bought them so he ate them. They had to be good things. In fact they were the best things he had ever eaten. It was wonderful walking with her, holding her hand. Then a truck with soldiers had passed, British soldiers, he knew. They were white soldiers. Everyone on the street was looking at the soldiers like creatures who were different and to be feared. Then he noticed that all the soldiers were looking at him. He was surprised. When he had seen British soldiers before he was sure that they never looked at anyone or anything. How was it they were looking at him? Ah, they were looking at his mother. But that was not strange, people always said his mother was the most beautiful woman and that she was the whitest woman in the world, that she was whiter than the white women. He had thought so too. Maybe that was why the soldiers looked. He felt proud and held his mother's fingers tighter. She was *his* mother. He was not afraid

11

of the soldiers any more; they were like everybody else. They actually saw people.

The yard in which he stayed was near a small river. During the day he would press his nose to the wire fence and stare into this river and at the people in the boats moving on the water. The fence of the yard seemed very high. There were always lots of animals in the yard. He remembered pigs, lots of pigs and sheep, and fowls and ducks. These always appeared to be in front of the large space in front of the house, and this large space had not a speck of green. There was something familiar. It was his first awareness of memory. In a flash this view of the bank of the Canje creek recalled the yard in Alexander Village in Demerara -- when he was about five.

At that time they were living in Oliver Street. It was more like an alley. A very wide alley. It was virtually enclosed on all sides, a self-contained world. In fact, until he was about six years old, Oliver Street *was* the world for Dalip. There were many boys in Oliver Street. Roy, his elder brother and Dhani, their cousin, who were both about four years older than Dalip, always seemed to head this group of boys. Dalip tagged along. He had to do whatever the boys did and whenever the boys did something mischievous, which they did most of the time, he knew he must not tell.

By nature he was not given to talking so he was accepted by the older boys, but Romesh, who talked a lot, was excluded whenever possible. It was always exciting when the boys were around, especially during the holidays when the grownups were away at work and they were by themselves.

One day Dhani suggested the idea of smoking. There were no cigarettes. For almost a week they thought about the problem. Still they could not get cigarettes. Then somebody said that they should try newspapers. One midmorning when all was clear they got matches and newspaper, rolled up the newspaper like giant cigars and took turns in the latrine. Two persons were always on guard in the event any elderly person came home unexpectedly. The newspaper did not work well. The paper went out quickly after being lit. Then it was remembered that tobacco was used in cigarettes. Tobacco was actually ground leaves. There were lots of dried leaves from the numerous vines in the yard. Dried leaves were soon obtained, ground, and stuffed into newspaper and smoked. Almost everyone was satisfied with the results and everyone was excited the afternoon when the actual smoking was done. It was felt that something momentous was happening, at least Dalip thought so. There was further excitement when Dhani suggested that they try smoking some of the very thick and drying vines. They cut lengths from the bottom of the vines because they did not want anybody to suspect. But they had problems lighting these vines and when these vines were lit the smoke was strong, causing almost everyone to cough and eyes to water. They did not smoke after that.

Dhani and Dalip were cousins. Dhani's father and Dalip's mother were brother and sister. For a while they lived in the same house. While Dalip lived wholly downstairs, Dhani's living quarters were upstairs, though the kitchen everyone shared was downstairs. Walls made little difference to the boys who lived like brothers. At least Roy, Dalip's elder brother, and Dhani were almost always together. Just before Dalip's parents had removed from Oliver Street, Dhani and Roy had decided that they could draw and spent most of their time together sketching – but that was not for a while yet.

During the afternoons after school, and when their parents had come home, all the boys in the yard – there were only boys – went to learn Hindi. It was great fun singing a a e e u u – but nobody liked writing. The teacher was a stern old man and everyone was afraid of his harshness when he gave dictations. The boys led by Dhani and Roy always took their time to get to the 'bottom house' Hindi school. They played games on the way and chased each other. Dalip hardly understood what was happening but he went along with everything all the same. After a while, classes had almost always started when they arrived and this annoyed the teacher very much. Shortly after, for no reason that Dalip could understand, they had stopped going to the classes. In later years he had felt guilty about this

13

and even now he blamed himself for his limited knowledge of the language.

At school everybody always told Dalip that he was a dreamer and even now some of his friends asserted that he was impractical and an idealist. What was the first fantasy he could remember? He was just over five years old and they were living in Oliver Street. He had been going to a private preparatory school in the next street. He went only in the mornings. Romesh went with him. Somehow Dalip got the impression that some of the other pupils were very well off. There was one girl in particular who was very pretty. She was very fair – like his mother – and she combed or had her hair combed in curls. She was somewhat chubby and always gave Dalip the impression that she was soft. He used to enjoy touching her when he thought nobody was looking. Later he had begun to pinch her. He would dream of having secreted her into their home and having hidden her under the bed. He could touch her and pinch her to his heart's content. And he used to dream of living alone with his mother as a little boy and not having to share her with his brothers and father. He used to be glad whenever she would come home tired and ask him to massage her body. Every time he touched her bare calves he would experience a queer thrill and would fear that his mother, who at such times would lie on her belly, would turn around and find him enraptured, looking at her body. He used to be scared but thrilled.

But there were also times when his experience was about uncovering the truth. He remembered how Romesh and himself had found out that Roy used to trick them. They did not go to school in the afternoon, but Roy, who was attending primary school, did. Every afternoon before he left for school he would put them in bed and tell them that he was sure that they could not fall asleep before he reached school. It was great fun pretending that they had fallen asleep, but one day they heard a noise in the kitchen when he should have reached school. They had called out and Roy had started to laugh saying he knew that they could not fall asleep. Later, Romesh

14

and Dalip became suspicious and decided to see what Roy did in the kitchen when he made them close their eyes. The wall which separated their bedroom from the kitchen had knots in the wood. Romesh and Dalip forced a knot out of the wall, then fixed it in again. They realised that from that particular hole they could see most of the kitchen. The next day they waited for Roy to put them to bed. They pretended to be asleep immediately but quietly got off the bed, pulled out the knot and spied on Roy. Roy was quietly opening the cupboard. He took out the Ovaltine tin. Took a spoon and carefully opened it. He then shovelled spoonfuls of Ovaltine into his mouth. Romesh could not contain himself. He rushed into the kitchen. Dalip dashed in after him. Roy was surprised. Dalip could not help laughing. Romesh demanded Ovaltine. From that day Roy did not put them to bed anymore.

Shortly after, Dalip was transferred to a primary school, though Romesh still went to the preparatory school. Somehow everyone soon got the idea that Dalip was exceptionally good at school. He never knew why people thought so. *He* did not think so but whenever he took home examples of work he did in school, he would be made to feel a hero, especially by his mother. He remembered one end of year. Everyone was excited that it was end of term and they had been told that if a student did well he would be promoted. Roy was studying more at home, as was Dhani. Their excitement spread to Dalip. *He* did not know what tests he did but he had a vague sense that they were important. On the day when school closed for the holidays his teacher gave him a piece of paper to give his parents. He did not know how to read this paper, or what was inside but he knew that the paper was important and he got the impression that this paper was called a 'pass paper'. His teacher had smiled and said something nice to him when she gave him his 'pass paper'. He felt he must have done something well and he felt that that something had to do with the slip of paper. Going home that afternoon he felt proud.

As soon as he entered Oliver Street, a boy who was a friend of Roy took Dalip's 'pass paper' and read it. He smiled and started to jeer at Dalip, laughingly telling Dalip that he had failed. Dalip became worried. As soon as his mother came home from work she asked him for his 'pass paper'. Dalip gave it to her and waited, not knowing what to expect.

His mother smiled and hugged him and kissed him. She said that he had done very well, better than his brothers, and that he had come second in his class. She said that ice-cream would be bought for him as he deserved it. His father seemed displeased at this and did not seem to want to go and buy the ice-cream when Dalip's mother asked him. *How* the idea came to him he did not know, yet Dalip knew that money was not the problem but that his father was not pleased because it was he and not Romesh who had done well. For some time Dalip had had such suspicions about his father's feelings, but he had not been troubled by them. However, on the day when he took home his 'pass paper' he became acutely aware of the tension when his mother said he deserved ice-cream. There had seemed to be some sort of silence which was broken by Romesh saying he wanted ice-cream and shouting, 'Ice-cream, ice-cream...'

Some time after this incident they moved from Oliver Street to Margaret Street. Margaret Street was not far away and there they moved into their own newly built home. Before the house was completed, his father and uncle, who was the carpenter who built the house, used to sleep in it at nights. Every night Dalip was sent to sleep with them. He knew no reason why this was so but he was glad. The only thing he was scared of was walking from Oliver Street to Margaret Street.

There were no street lights in Margaret Street and sometimes dogs would chase him. The moon, when it was very huge and round, also made him scared. Every night he walked to Margaret Street with his sheet and pillow. When he reached the house his father and uncle were always there, sometimes with one or two other persons whom Dalip did not know. They would be doing something or other. He mostly remembered them fixing windows. They were always asking him to

16

bring the plane or saw or nails or rule or something or other. Dalip did not mind. Quite the opposite, he felt glad that he was helping. His father and uncle always had a bottle of what he suspected was rum. Whenever they spoke about anything he sensed that they spoke freely and were not bothered that he heard. At home, with his mother or other brothers around, they seemed more cautious. Dalip felt glad when they did not notice him. He would look closely at the odd jobs they did, but more absorbing and exciting were the elongated shadows made by the lamps on the walls, which made the house look so different at night. It was here for the first time that Dalip felt an attraction to his father.

When they moved into their new home Dalip was transferred to another primary school which was much nearer and Romesh, for the first time, was admitted to primary school. Normally it was their mother who looked after such business but on this occasion, for some unfathomable reason, their father looked after this affair which took till midmorning to be completed. Dalip saw a side of his father he had never seen before. His father was very polite with persons he came into contact with. With Romesh and Dalip he was gentle. He saw them settled into their classes. He instructed them how to get home at midday and told them that they should walk home together.

When they got home at midday, their father enquired how they had got along in school and he told them when to leave for the afternoon session. Now their father began to play a greater part in their lives. When they went home for lunch at midday their father would be at home from work for his lunch. He saw to it that Romesh and Dalip ate their lunches. Some middays when something was cooked which Romesh did not like, he would throw the food out of the window when their father was not around. Dalip never told on Romesh. Sometimes he would want to throw his food through the window too, but he was always scared that he would be caught. One day Romesh had to force curry into the pocket of his pants because, as he was about to throw it through the window, their father appeared. Dalip had a good laugh later.

In the afternoons their mother's presence was felt. Once she came home from work, the house had a different atmosphere. At midday there was an aura of indolence but once their mother came home the house had greater life. She seemed always to be cleaning, arranging and rearranging, cooking and sending them on various errands. Dalip always found that there was something to do. Lately too, he had started to become scared of his mother, especially when Roy did anything wrong and she would scold him or sometimes hit him. Dalip made sure that *he* did everything exactly as she told him.

There were many times, however, when he was pleased to be in her company, such as on Sunday mornings when she would take Romesh and him on her cycle to the mandir, or on special occasions when she would take them at nights. She would also take him and Romesh to the mandir to pray whenever it was their birthdays. Romesh never wanted to go, but Dalip, whilst not caring to go in the daytime, loved it at night.

When they moved into the house in Margaret Street, on holidays and some weekends the house seemed filled with relatives. There would be singing and dancing and music – all Indian, of course. Their mother would have nothing else. The house then was always noisy and happy and Dalip felt happy even though he, Roy and Romesh had to be at the back of the house, out of sight; but they saw and always strained to hear from their bedroom what was going on. Romesh and Dalip would take turns peeping at the gay scene. Dalip always admired his mother floating among the guests, offering them this or that, chatting with them and making everyone laugh.

Occasionally on Sunday mornings they would all go to the seaside to bathe. Dalip sensed that his mother was responsible for this. She was a splendid swimmer. Dalip was always scared of the water but he tried to pretend not to be because he was afraid that his mother would be displeased with him if he showed fear. His father was also a strong swimmer but he almost always remained with them at the edge of the water. It was on such occasions that Dalip always felt some kinship with his father but the moment his mother came close he transferred his feelings to her. Sometimes, he found himself forced (by what he did not know) to side with her against his father. Not openly, of course. At times he felt there was some tension between his parents — but his mother was so beautiful.

Once in the country when they visited his father's sister, they all went picnicking near the sea. All the elders went swimming in a huge canal; the children kept to the edge of the bank or stayed on the dam looking at the older folks swimming. When his mother put on her bathing suit everyone stared at her. She was so beautiful and so white. Dalip, who was playing at the edge of the canal, came out and sat on the dam admiring her like all the other children and all the older people — relatives and bystanders. Her body shot smoothly through the air and she was in the water. She out-swam everybody present — male and female. It was a joy to Dalip to watch her slender athletic arms as she swam. When she did the backswim, she was like a queen. She moved like an aeroplane and all the swimmers paused in awe to watch her.

On another occasion Dalip's father had borrowed his friend's car and along with his elder brother (Dalip's Cha Cha), his wife and children, who crammed themselves into the car, they went to one of the creeks on a picnic. This creek was some twenty-seven miles out of the city and not far from the Atkinson International Airbase. They had a most wonderful outing. From early in the morning Dalip's father and mother were cooking and preparing for the trip. As the sun peeped over the horizon Dalip's father returned after filling up the car with petrol. They piled in after packing baskets into the trunk. Then they collected Dalip's Mamoo (his mother's youngest brother), then his Cha Cha, his wife and Dalip's cousins. Dalip hardly met with his cousins because they lived in the heart of the city and far from each other. Their merely being together was an event. They were constantly talking and laughing throughout the trip.

They sang on the way; helped in turn by Dalip's father and his brother, their Cha Cha, who sang with great skill,

19

Dalip thought, both Indian songs and songs in English. He particularly loved classical songs – especially those sung by Bing Crosby, Mario Lanza and Frank Sinatra. They had one puncture but instead of dampening their spirits it made them happier. At least Dalip felt that his brothers and cousins felt so. While the spare was being put on they stretched their legs on the parapet and waved to passing people. At last they arrived at the creek.

In a flash Dalip's mother seemed to overshadow everyone else: at the creek bathing and swimming, after they had changed and the food was being served and during the singing. Dalip felt he loved his mother very much then. He admired her for her ability to make everyone happy. He was proud that she was his mother and he tended to sense that everyone in their group felt happy to be associated with her. There was great laughter and much excitement when it was found that she had forgotten to put salt in one of the dishes. The food was eaten all the same. In fact, long after the trip, this became a point of reference and a happy reminder.

Neither Dalip, Roy or Romesh liked their father when it came to deciding where or how long they would spend their August vacation. They sensed that their father did not want them to spend a holiday anywhere except at home. In the end their mother prevailed. She was the champion for relaxation and entertainment. That first year when they moved into their Margaret Street home they spent their holidays with their mother's father, their mother's stepmother and her stepbrothers. Roy, Dalip and Romesh enjoyed these holidays.

When their mother and father had taken them to their maternal grandfather, who lived out of Georgetown on the East Bank of the Demerara River, everyone was glad to have them. That was the first time Dalip remembered meeting his mother's father. Two months almost seemed to melt away in seconds. There was always something to do – something novel. Their step-uncles ranged in ages, the youngest and Dalip being of the same age, while the eldest was about four years older than Roy. There were four uncles and an aunt. And she seemed to adore her nephews. Dalip always remembered her making some sweetmeat or other almost every day, mostly Indian sweetmeats, some of which were Dalip's favourites, and others he had never heard of or eaten before.

When Dalip's two elder uncles had time, they were always taking Romesh, Roy and himself cycling. They took them to their farm some two miles away. This was all new to Dalip. They went picking peaches from trees which seemed so loaded that the branches bent close to the ground. That was the first time Dalip remembered eating peaches. At first he did not like them, but afterwards grew to enjoy these fruits. Often in the peach season they would go and pick large bags of peaches which were sorted and then sold. Of course, they had peaches at home in abundance. Later, during the same holiday, guineps were in season. His uncles climbed the massive trees and picked the fruits which were placed in buckets and lowered slowly to the ground with very long pieces of rope.

Sometimes they were taken to the riverside. This was fun. There was a lot of mud, especially when the tide was out, but this made crab-catching more enjoyable. Then there were sessions when they shot down doves with slingshots.

When this was discovered by their eldest uncle he scolded the brother who had taken Dalip, Roy and Romesh shooting doves. There were fierce quarrels between Dalip's two uncles on this issue, one claiming that it was a sin to shoot doves, the other arguing fiercely against this. Dalip never quite followed the argument of the dove-shooting uncle, though he supported him because he found dove-shooting exciting. Dalip's eldest uncle was a staunch Christian. Dalip got the impression that he used to preach, at any rate he used to sing and play the guitar. He took Dalip along with him when he went to church at night, which was at least once a week and, when there were crusades, almost every night. Dalip didn't really understand what was going on, but he enjoyed especially the open-air crusades at nights. He loved being in what, he fancied, was a tremendous crowd. He loved the singing and clapping and rhythms of the electric guitars and the drum-sets.

21

He loved the fiery speeches and talk of God and Jesus Christ and most of all he loved seeing the foreign preachers in their collars and ties and hearing their strangely musical English with the unfamiliar accent. These foreign or guest preachers were mostly Americans but some were British.

He was also taken to the nearby mandir by his grandfather who had come from India as an indentured immigrant in the early part of the century. He knew Hindi. He read it and spoke it. Every night Dalip would observe his grandfather reverently uncover his *Ramayana*, which was always wrapped in red cotton, and read silently for an hour or two. His grandfather would then carefully rewrap the volume and place it on his shelf. At such times Dalip would contemplate his grandfather in awe and respect but always wondered what he found so interesting. On many occasions, by the time his grandfather was finished, everyone except Dalip would be in bed. After the first week his grandfather would permit Dalip to sit close to him as he read. So it was that Dalip knew that the book was in Hindi, for he recognised the letters he had started to learn at Hindi classes when they were living in Oliver Street. He wished, at such times, he had learnt his Hindi so that he could read what his grandfather read.

However, when his grandfather started taking him to the mandir, Dalip was familiar with what happened because he had often gone with his mother. Roy was never really interested and Romesh only went because of the tasty *prasad* which was distributed at the end of each service. Dalip liked it too, as he liked the singing of *bhajans* and the playing of the harmonium and the *dhantal*, but he also liked to feel part of the congregation, which he did, even though he knew nobody there. Here everybody sat on the ground and left his or her shoes and slippers outside. It was like being at home – no, it **was** being at home. Everyone was a stranger yet a relative – everyone was of his kind. He loved, too, to see the girls with their *orhanis* draped over their shoulders or head; they looked almost as beautiful as his mother looked when she wore her *orhani*.

Dalip noted that his grandfather rarely spoke but, when he did, Dalip loved to hear his voice which was full, heavy, musical and very throaty. During his stay with his grandfather he never once heard him say anything bad about Christianity, or Islam for that matter. In fact, he had never heard his grandfather utter a single word about Christianity or reproach his sons for following Christ. Dalip could not understand it, particularly when he heard his uncle make slighting remarks about Hinduism and sometimes openly attacked his father's religion.

Although Dalip was somewhat scared of his grandfather he felt him to be correct. Dalip liked his uncle very much, he was always kind and generally considerate – except when he attacked his father and Hinduism – yet he felt without knowing why, that his uncle was wrong. Yet he still went to church with his uncle and to the mandir with his grandfather.

Two months ended. He was sad to leave it all behind but glad that he would be with his mother again. He had hardly missed her during the two months.

School reopened. Things went on as before, but before long Dalip seemed to sense a change somewhere, though he could not place it. Prior to the holidays his father had always come home late at least one afternoon a week – usually Saturdays. His mother never liked this but she hardly seemed to say anything about it. After the holidays Dalip realised that his father was coming home late at least two days each week, Saturdays as usual and some other day, which never seemed fixed. He was then always under the influence of alcohol. Then Dalip would feel for his mother. He knew that Roy and Romesh felt just as much too. Whenever their father came home late during the week, the boys would go downstairs. There would be a row between their parents, though the boys hardly heard the words of the rows because their mother always closed the door of her bedroom.

Roy, Dalip and Romesh would loiter under the house sullen and silent. Dalip would strain to catch words. Sometimes there were sounds like blows. Then he hated his father.

He sensed that Roy and even Romesh felt so too. At such times he felt like murdering him.

From then onwards, whenever during the week their father stayed out late, the boys found themselves drawn to their mother. They were tender with her. They felt her hurting. They had to show her that although they could not understand what was happening, they knew that something was happening. After a while she seemed to understand and then it did not seem to bother her as much as before. She seemed her old self, her spirit, indomitable – lively as ever, gay as ever. She seemed to draw courage when she recognised that her sons sympathised with *her*. Dalip realised that she had started to take greater interest in Roy's and his own schoolwork. If their teacher told them to ask their parents buy some new text book, their father would grumble. When they told their mother, they never knew how she did it, but the very next day she would buy the book. Sometimes their father would say that he checked and could not get the book. Their mother always got the book.

Whenever their father was late, they would all sit downstairs waiting, after they had finished eating their dinner. Their mother would put on the downstairs light and they would sit around it. Then their mother would ask each of them in turn what he wanted to become when he grew up. Roy would say that he wanted to become a doctor. She would smile and approve. Dalip never knew what to say. He did not know what she would approve of. At first he used to hesitate, then she would prompt him. What about a lawyer? Yes, he would say. He would become a lawyer. He was never sure what he wanted to become, but whenever she asked he said, a lawyer. She approved. Romesh would say that he wanted to become a manager. She indicated approval, but Dalip sensed that she did not really like that. She never disapproved, probably because Romesh was always so emphatic in his choice. She would always impress upon the boys that they should study hard and become important men, that one of them should go away to some foreign country and study. She always insisted on England. All of this became routine whenever their father was late. Yet no matter how many times they went through this, each time their mother imbued them with a stronger feeling that they should become what they said they wanted to become in life. After each session Dalip became more and more convinced that he had to become somebody – if only for his mother's sake.

The more Dalip's father stayed away from home, the more Dalip's mother attached herself to her sons. This was not new, but perhaps only that Dalip felt the attachment more. So too Dalip noticed her increased religiosity, though again his mother had always been a very religious woman. She'd had an altar built in the corner of the house, (by Dalip's father who, though he never seemed religious, would be present often on Sundays when the family prayed together and sang *bhajans*) and she prayed, she fasted regularly and she still went to the mandir on occasions. At one level, life in the home seemed to be going on as usual. There were the usual visits by aunts and uncles and relatives and friends; there continued to be happy social gatherings. But at the back of his mind Dalip sensed some tension, from what, he was never quite sure, except that it had to do with his father. At times, when he was by himself, he would think that if he had a wife like his mother he would worship her as they worshipped the Goddess Saraswattie. *He* would be sure to come home on time. He would never drink rum. He would pray with her and go to the mandir with her, he would love her more than anything else, more than himself. Dalip had never once seen his father go into the mandir nor had he heard anyone refer to any time when his father had done so.

At times Dalip got the impression that his father deliberately did things to hurt his mother. Apart from the rum, his father consumed beef. His father knew how religious his mother was, how orthodox, how Hindu, (not that he himself was anything else – he too came from a very religious home and later, to his great surprise, Dalip learnt that his parents first saw each other at a Hindi school in their youth – and the

25

teacher was his father, his mother one of the pupils!) yet his father deliberately ate beef, the eating of which was considered *chamar* and unhindu. Dalip did not know why at the time. Sometimes his father wanted his beef prepared on Sundays – the day his mother would fast and do her puja – and he always seemed happy when the boys ate beef; even Dalip ate it too. He felt some curiosity; to him it was like the smoking adventures he had been involved in when they lived in Oliver Street; something which he knew to be wrong yet which he had to try and which he tried because he was certain he would get away with the act. But Dalip felt guilty about it because he knew that his mother never ate beef.

That his mother loved his father very much Dalip was convinced. This hurt and puzzled him, especially when Dalip knew his father did many things his mother did not like and, he felt, his father did those things deliberately. Whenever his father wanted beef to eat his mother always prepared it. Wordlessly, meekly. Sometimes Dalip hoped that his mother would refuse, sometimes he expected her to refuse but she never did. It was on these occasions that Dalip started to realise how much his mother loved his father and that his father knew this. And he sensed that his father loved his mother too, but wanted, it appeared, to give some other impression. He knew *that* on Sunday mornings when, regardless of the tension during the week concerning his lateness after work, his father would join them at the altar during the puja. Sometimes Dalip sensed that it was his father's way of saying sorry.  He loved his father then. Whenever that happened Dalip felt everyone was happy in the house. Occasionally, his father would come home early every day of the week. Everybody would be at ease then. Dalip thought that home must be like heaven.

Dalip loved his father too for his generosity where money was concerned. He knew that his father and mother disagreed on this issue. He had often heard his mother tell his father that the boys should not get accustomed to spending, as it was a bad habit, and she instructed him to give Dalip and Romesh a penny spending money only on three days of each week,

Mondays, Wednesdays and Fridays. Dalip always made do with his money. A penny was a lot of money for him and he sometimes managed to put something in his saving cup. Romesh, on the other hand, never seemed able to make his money do, so at middays he would ask their father. Their mother never came home for lunch. At first their father was hesitant, but then he started to give both boys a penny and warned them not to tell their mother. He need not have said that because both knew that if their mother found out not only would she row with their father but that both of them would get a spanking. It became a secret between Romesh, Dalip and their father. The boys felt closer to him after this. Sometimes they would compete with each other for his attention when he came home early from work.

At Diwali that year, which was in late October, there was a lot of cleaning up done around the house. On the day itself which was a public holiday, even their father helped their mother. The boys felt happy because they knew that everything was well with their parents. The diyas were washed – all the boys had to bathe and their father helped supervise their dressing while their mother completed the cooking. Romesh, Dalip and Roy were in good spirits because they knew that there would be a lot of sweet things for them to eat. Roy and their mother went to the mandir to make an offering. When they returned their mother started putting oil in all the diyas and making wicks. Their father helped too; this made everyone happy. Then the whole family gathered before the altar and there was a puja after which a diya was lit. As the place got darker all the diyas were lit and the boys and their father, under the direction of their mother, placed the lighted diyas in different places. This was fun for the boys. When they were finished, as a group, they gazed at their handiwork. Their parents were standing close together. The boys rushed up to them, holding one or the other or both and, like them, looked at the lighted diyas. It was a beautiful sight. Then they went out on their bridge and looked at the other houses and yards which were lit up. Then they saw the fireworks in all colours high in the sky, way in the distance, coming from the direction where the Diwali fair was being held. Soon the wind started to blow out some of the diyas. Roy, Dalip and Romesh raced and competed with each other to relight them. In the meantime lots of people had appeared on their bridges looking at the other lighted yards; there seemed to be crowds of people walking round inspecting and admiring. Dalip could not remember experiencing anything like this before, and at night too. This made the festival more awesome and mysterious for him.

When they went back into the house their mother served the various things she had prepared. There seemed to be so much, everything was sweet and there was no meat. After eating they crowded around their parents, playing with them until they felt sleepy and were put to bed. They all said their customary evening prayers aloud – *twamewanata cha pita twameva, twameva bandhushcha sakhaa twameva, twameva vidyaa dravinam- twameva, twameva sarvam mama deva deva* – before bidding their parents goodnight.

The next day was not a working day. The boys woke up feeling happy and brightly bid their mother and father, 'Ram, Ram', as they had been trained to do by their mother for as long as they could remember. She was already up and cleaning up the house and oil stains made by the diyas, collecting the diyas and washing them. The boys had a good breakfast because there was lots of sweet food left over from the previous night. They too, almost unasked, helped their mother to collect the diyas lit the night before, as their father was doing. After lunch their father played music on the tape recorder. Everything seemed festive. That night their parents and their uncles and aunts would be going to the Diwali fair. Dalip did not mind being left at home because he sensed that his parents would be happy if they went to the fair without having to look after them. On their own, the boys sang loudly all the songs they knew and even those they did not know fully – here they invented their own 'Hindi' words to keep the tunes going. They beat on the bedstead and made merry until they dropped to sleep. Dalip did not know when his parents came home but it had to be very late that night – or very early in the morning.

They gathered that their parents had enjoyed themselves. When their aunts and uncles visited afterwards they made constant references to the fair, and straining to overhear from their bedroom Dalip was able to understand that there had been some Indian dancing competition, a sari fashion show and a singing competition. His father and uncles constantly spoke of the competition. His father, who it seemed knew the top singer of the city and who had sung with him long ago on a number of occasions, had won the competition. It appeared that many persons who had travelled from the country areas thought that another singer should have won, had started throwing rum bottles and fights had broken out.

There was another occasion when the whole family was happy. That was during Christmas. On Christmas eve their parents had bought, it seemed to Dalip, many, many things. His mother seemed to be very busy. When their father came home he too seemed busy and he helped their mother. Then he left to borrow a friend's car. The boys were very excited because he had promised to take them downtown on Christmas Eve, to see Santa Claus and to buy toy pistols and shots for them. Their mother bathed and dressed them in their best clothing. When she was nearly finished their father returned with a car. He bathed and shaved and dressed. He looked handsome and for the first time Dalip felt his father suited his mother, who looked as beautiful as ever.

They set off for the shopping centre of the city which looked like some of the pictures Dalip had seen in his story books. There were lights everywhere, lights on strings. Some were small lights like peppers blinking on and off in many colours, while some of the lights on string were bulbs like those in their house, but in a variety of colours. There were strings of these bulbs on almost all the huge trees near the Public Library. Their father said that the street was Main Street. There were problems parking the car. There seemed to be cars everywhere; stationary ones and moving ones. There were crowds of people moving in two streams on the pavements, two opposing and unending streams. There were many boys and girls with their parents, with parcels in their hands – and like him they were all dressed up. The pavement was littered with torn gift-wrapping paper, the discarded wrappings of 'caps' and strings of used 'caps' curling like little pink snakes on the ground. All this gave the early evening a festive atmosphere. Then there were the sounds of car horns, of a variety of toy guns, squibs and, from the huge and brightly lit stores, there was the sound of Christmas carols.

Dalip was frightened that he might get lost in the immense crowd so he held tightly to Roy. They went into a big store where they saw lots of toys and chairs, clothing and just about everything that Dalip could think of. While they were in the elevator Dalip felt scared again. He had seen people go into this iron thing which was closed after them and disappeared with them. He had never been in an elevator before. However, he didn't say anything because his parents and brother appeared so calm and he was afraid they would say he was a coward. Before he realised it the elevator had returned and he was being ushered in.

It was small and overcrowded. Dalip wanted to shout when the door closed. It seemed he would be suffocated. He held onto his father's legs; his mother patted him. There was a bump, the door opened and they were out in another part of the store. Dalip felt relieved. There was a line to see Santa Claus and Roy, Dalip and Romesh joined it. There were many children opening packages which Santa had given them. Dalip saw guns, cars, buses, trucks, games, toy tools and many other things which excited him. Their father disappeared but their mother remained with them. Then it was Dalip's turn; Santa said something nice to him and held him. Dalip felt happy. Santa was just like Dalip had seen him on postcards and in the newspaper. He had a long white beard, black boots, wore a flowing red robe and his skin was white. Dalip got his gift. This was a car which sounded like a police car when you pushed it. He was pleased, as were Romesh and Roy, with the toys they got.

By then their father reappeared with ice-cream cones for them. They were taken to another similar store and their father told them to choose the type of guns they wanted. Roy chose a shiny gun in a holster. It was heavy but he managed it easily. It was a beautiful gun, Dalip thought, and both he and Romesh said they wanted similar guns, but when their father gave them similar guns they could barely lift them, nor could they pull the triggers. Roy laughed at them, their father too. Dalip felt like crying and Romesh had started to insist that he wanted a gun like Roy's. But their mother lifted him up and showed him other guns. He soon forgot Roy's, as did Dalip. Smaller guns were bought for them, similar to each other. Sulphur shots were bought – a whole box full – and the boys were anxious to get home and try the guns. Dalip did not care about the night, the lights, the people anymore. All he wanted was to get home to try shooting his gun.

When they arrived home, they had to wait for their father to return his friend's car then walk home, to show them how to operate their guns. Their mother in the meantime had finished seasoning a chicken which she put into the oven to bake. When their father returned home all the boys crowded around him, each one of them wanted to be the first to be shown how to operate his gun. Roy did not have to be shown; he already knew but he still wanted their father to fix his gun first. After being shown how to fix their guns they could not restrain themselves, they started shooting their guns, aiming at one another. Dalip ran into the kitchen to display his gun to his mother with Romesh after him. They pointed their guns at her and pulled the triggers, then they pretended to shoot each other. When their mother called them for cakes and drinks and nuts they did not go. Their father told her to keep it for later. Their father helped Roy fix his holster. Roy then began prac-tising to 'draw' his gun quickly. Soon Dalip and Romesh were imitating him. They had to be content with sticking their guns in their waistbands because their guns were not sold with holsters. Dalip and Romesh together counted to three, drew their guns and shot at each other. Soon there were disputes – each claiming to have shot first. Their father intervened. He started to do the counting and he judged who shot first.

Then their father, egged on by Roy, had them play as cowboys in battle. Their father would be on one side and they on the other. They kept this up for quite a while, their father staying at one end of the house and the boys at the other. At first their father won most of the encounters but as they got the idea of what to do the boys began to win.

Then their mother laughingly told the boys that they were taking advantage of their father and she took him into the kitchen to show him something. Now it was Romesh and Dalip against Roy. They played many games. Sometimes Roy won, sometimes Dalip and Romesh. They played until their mother announced that the chicken was finished.

They sprinted into the kitchen. The chicken looked delicious – as delicious as Dalip had seen in his picture books. Their father had them put up their guns. He said that they had had enough for one night, that they would have all of the next day, Christmas, and the next day, Boxing day, and the remainder of the holidays. They reluctantly put away their guns. Their mother made them wash and they sat down to the baked chicken, cake and various kinds of drink. After they finished they chatted with their parents who after a while sent them to bed. Dalip noted that his parents seemed to have something in mind. He did not want to go to bed yet, but he got the impression that his parents wanted to be alone.

The next day -- Christmas – was a very busy day. Again their mother was up early cooking. The boys got up early too, shooting their guns. By ten o'clock the house started to fill up. Dalip's Cha Cha and his cousins arrived. His aunt Coreen, his Cha Cha's wife, and her daughters, Dalip's cousins, remained with his mother helping, but Dalip's male cousins and Roy and Romesh had the whole yard to themselves. They played at cowboys – his cousins brought their guns too. Shortly afterwards, the uncle who had been the carpenter-contractor of the house arrived with his family; again all the boys joined together. The games of cowboys and soldiers continued now on a grander scale.

Then there was a break for lunch. The boys did not mind lunch. It was a rare thing to meet together like that. When they trooped upstairs the house seemed overflowing. The boys took up various positions in the kitchen and ate. The music coming from the front of the house was loud and rollicking – Indian songs and music mostly. The men seemed to be discussing something very interesting. Voices could be heard above the music. Dalip was curious. He wanted to know what they were talking about. The girls were whispering and laughing. They were playing some game with dice. Through it all shone his mother. She was at ease. She was happy and she made everyone else feel happy. She moved from group to group. Enquiring, offering this or that, giving one instruction or another.

Dalip did not want to go downstairs with the rest of the boys who seemed impatient to get back to their games. He would have liked to stay upstairs and follow the conversations of his father and uncles. He knew that the liquor flowed like the conversation but this did not bother him. He accepted that his father and uncles could only be happy if there was alcohol around, even though he did not like his father drinking alcohol. However, Dalip knew that if he remained upstairs the other boys would call him a 'sissy'.

The boys led by Roy, instead of confining themselves and their war games to the yard, now used the whole length of Margaret Street and the alley. Later they were called in for cakes, drinks, nuts and sweets. The boys raced to see who would be fastest at cracking the almond-nuts and walnuts. They helped the girls crack theirs. They used a hammer, stones, heavy bits of wood and gun butts.

Then to accommodate the girls they played doll-house – acting as mothers and fathers and policemen, soldiers and sons and daughters. This was done very seriously. Then someone suggested hide-and-seek. The seeker would count to one hundred while the others hid themselves. The first person found would be the seeker for the next round. The girls were mostly the seekers as they were generally found first. The boys found the most unusual places and competed to see who could find the most difficult spots. When the girls left the boys, the game was extended out of the yard and this made the game very exciting.

Then the boys were called to bathe. They trooped into the bathroom downstairs in sets according to age group, without anybody asking or telling them to. They splashed and wet each other. Dalip, Romesh and the younger boys wanted to bathe in the open at the washstand but the girls were standing on the platform and would have seen them – and made fun of them. After their baths and redressing, the boys were given another snack. They felt clean and did not feel up to their games which would have made them untidy again. Then, too, they had not realised that time had passed so quickly; it was after four and they would have to separate in another three or four hours. They did not know when they would meet together like that again. They just sat on the platform, stairway and rails and talked. Roy and the older boys took the lead. They spoke about amusing or unpleasant incidents at school. The girls contributed also. There were suggestions about girl-friends and boyfriends. The girls went in to help with dinner and films became the topic.

When the boys were called in to dinner it was getting dark. They were sad at having to part but their good moods returned when they were all asked to go in front where their fathers and other male relatives were. Everybody gathered there. They sat on chair handles, on the floor, near to parents or aunts. Dalip sat on his Cha Cha's lap. He liked him very much. Then dinner was served. Even Dalip's mother ate too and they were happy. Dalip was asked by his Mamoo how he was getting along in school. He found it difficult to speak. The boys started to laugh. He found his voice and stammered, 'Al... al... right.' There was more laughter.

During the course of dinner his uncle who was the carpenter announced that the next day – Boxing Day – would be spent at his home. The boys almost simultaneously started shouting joyfully. Romesh, with his plate in one hand, jumped onto the chair with it. Guns appeared from nowhere and there was lots of shooting.

The day before Old Year's, Roy, Dalip, Romesh and their parents were relaxing together, as they sometimes did before going to bed. Their mother was leafing through an embroidery magazine, flanked by Romesh and Dalip. Roy was reading a book and their father a novel. Their mother turned pages rather quickly. She stopped suddenly and said, 'Terry....' She did not continue. Dalip hardly ever heard his mother call his father by this name. Dalip knew that this was not his father's real name. It was the name he had been called since he was a boy. Something was wrong, he sensed. His mother's voice was tender, yet it sounded uncharacteristically sad, as though she was begging for something. Dalip thought he saw something correspondingly tender in his father's glance. He also looked slightly surprised. His father closed the book.

'Is something wrong Sav... ?' Dalip was surprised. It was the first time he heard his father call his mother Sav – short for Savitri.

'I was thinking that we should spend Old Year's and New Year's at Talbot,' she answered. Dalip's Cha Cha was called Talbot.

'Why?' Dalip's father sounded genuinely surprised, his question even harsh. He continued, 'Since we've been married we've never once spent a New Year's out of home. You yourself... Why?'

'Coreen...' was all his mother said. Dalip felt her arm tighten around him. 'Coreen has cancer.'

'What!' his father almost shouted. 'How do you know? Since when?'

His mother seemed to have regained control over herself.

'She told me on Christmas Day. The doctor told her two days before. Talbot doesn't know yet. He will take it hard. She will have to tell him after New Year. She said if she had told

35

him before Christmas it would spoil everything, the whole holidays. I think so too. You understand?' There was a very long silence. Dalip's parents looked at each other for a long time.

'Yes Sav... We will spend Old Year's and New Year's at my brother. Terrible... How long?'

'Later.' His mother looked at him. Dalip saw his father nodding.

'Thanks, Terry.'

'No. Thanks, Sav.' Almost immediately after they all went to bed. Dalip hardly understood what happened. To him his mother had asked his father to spend Old Year's and New Year's at his Cha Cha's. His father was angry at first then he agreed because of something to do with aunt Coreen. Dalip was glad but something puzzled him. Something which he could not understand.

# Chapter Two

In January it was confirmed that Dalip's Cha Cha's wife, aunt Coreen, was suffering from cancer. The fact was not hidden any longer. Dalip did not really understand what this cancer was all about. He knew it was something bad. Then he started to hear from various sources, mostly relatives who visited and discussed the topic with his parents, that it was a sickness for which there was no known or complete cure, that the victim always died in the end. He learnt that this sickness fed on the patient, 'ate' the organs and that it was like the branches of a tree growing and spreading, until it took over the whole of the patient or damaged some vital part of the body. Dalip's mother spent a lot of time with his aunt Coreen. From conversations Dalip learnt that various specialists were being consulted. He also gathered that she would have to go away for some treatment. Dalip noticed that though his mother was just as considerate and tender as before, and sometimes as lively, there was something that seemed always to be bothering her. Dalip sensed this more than observed it. He felt this even though it appeared as though his mother was the same. He felt that it had to do with his aunt Coreen. It seemed that after his mother's conversation with his father before Old Year's day this *something* started bothering her. This was what led him to suspect that it was because aunt Coreen was sick.

Then one afternoon -- it seemed like a Sunday to Dalip -- his father borrowed his friend's car and took them all to his Cha Cha. When they arrived, his Cha Cha, aunt Coreen and his cousins were waiting. They all piled into the car. Dalip supposed they were all going for an afternoon drive. They left Georgetown and drove along a road which seemed familiar to him. He felt ill at ease. There was constant lively chatter among his cousins, Romesh and Roy and occasionally among his parents, his Cha Cha and aunt Coreen, yet somehow he felt some constriction among them, some inhibition and this affected him. He found it difficult to be as lively as his cousins, Roy and Romesh. He kept looking outside trying to give the impression that he was admiring the countryside – which was to some extent true – but actually he was trying to hide an oppressive sadness that seemed to be stifling him and trying to remember why the countryside seemed familiar. Then he heard someone in front say, 'The last time we travelled this way we had a wonderful time. I shall never forget it...' The voice broke off. The voice sounded faraway. Dalip could not tell if it was because of the laughing of Roy and his cousins that the voice sounded low or because it was actually said in a low tone. Dalip strained to hear what was being said by the elders in front. For quite some time there seemed to be silence. Dalip started to wonder if he had actually heard the statement or imagined it. It had been a woman's voice but he could not tell if it was his mother's or aunt Coreen's.

'We're going by the air base, aren't we, mommy?' Dalip shouted. He remembered now. When they had gone picnicking near the creek, this was where they had travelled. He did not realise that he had almost shouted until his cousins and brothers started laughing at him.

'You didn't know that?' jeered Romesh.

'He was in dreamland,' teased Roy. He remembered that his aunt Coreen turned around and smiled at him.

Her smile seemed to tell him that she understood how he felt because he was being laughed at. When they reached near the air base, his father, who was driving, said he would take them for a drive on the tracks where the car and motorcycle races were held. Dalip felt happy. He had heard his friends in school talk of the races at the circuit and how the cars and motor-cycles went into the 'Goose neck' and how sometimes motorcyclists rode off the track at this point. His father raced the car on the track, and it seemed to tilt dangerously when he

38

went through the 'Goose neck' and Dalip felt pleasurably excited.

Then the car had stopped and they came out into some building. Dalip did not remember what exactly happened. But there seemed to be hugging and kissing and he thought he saw his mother sobbing silently. He thought there were tears in her eyes but he could not be certain because of her spectacles. He was baffled. He was under the impression that they were going for a drive. Then he remembered seeing his parents and his Cha Cha waving. When he followed the direction of their stares, he saw to his surprise, aunt Coreen in the distance going up a stairway into a big aeroplane. He remembered that she paused just before going into the plane. She seemed to have stopped there for some time. She waved. Dalip's parents waved, his Cha Cha waved, his brothers waved, his cousins waved. He found himself waving. After some time the plane started making a loud noise, then it started to move slowly, like a worm, he thought. It disappeared from sight. Nobody moved or said anything. They seemed to be waiting for something. Dalip said nothing and waited like them. He saw a blur. He heard Romesh or somebody shout, 'Look! Look! Very fast....' The plane flashed past and rose into the air.

Nobody said much on the drive back to the city. Dalip felt very tired and he thought everybody else must be feeling so too. When they reached Georgetown it was dark. The lights were on but to Dalip the city seemed darker than on Christmas Eve night and the pavements were almost deserted. The city looked frightening and suddenly he felt scared of the city and the night – for the first time that he could recall – he felt scared of the darkness. He felt so tired. He was glad to be back home.

Life continued as normal except that his mother and father went out frequently together. They never said where they were going but Dalip and Roy would try to guess. Roy always insisted that their parents went to their Cha Cha's.

Dalip thought that his mother was becoming increasingly irritable. She seemed to be at home more often from work. He did not know why.    It seemed that his parents were waiting for something and this appeared to be affecting his mother in some strange way. Overnight she seemed to have become a very stern woman and Dalip started to feel scared of her. She would be harsh with them at times and hit them if they did something she did not like, especially Roy who always seemed to be getting a blow from her with whatever she happened to have in her hand. Dalip noticed that Roy was scared of his mother too and would be nervous whenever she asked him to do anything.

Dalip was surprised at his father's reaction to all this. He accepted it all; he never said a word even when she was harsh with him. Normally he would not tolerate her speaking harshly to him in front of Dalip, Roy or Romesh. Normally, that only happened, the boys believed, behind the closed door of their parents' bedroom.

Dalip's mother seemed to have stopped working. Then it was said she would have to go to Berbice for some 'treatment' to help her health. Roy went with her. They would be going to Canje and would stay where Dalip had stayed when he had gone to Berbice with her, when they had been living in Oliver Street.

Dalip and Romesh stayed with a neighbour until their father came home from work. The neighbour would make porridge much thicker than they were accustomed to – it was as thick and as firm as jelly – when they came home from school. They liked eating it with milk, which she would pour liberally over this 'porridge'. Their house seemed empty now. Both Dalip and Romesh were scared of the house and the yard. Both seemed so deserted. They missed Roy very much. Now they realised how much they depended on him. If ever they had cause to go in their yard for anything before their father came home, they would hurry and do it and when they were finished they would sprint back to the safety of their neighbour's kitchen.

School seemed to have closed for August, because they were not going to school, nor was anyone else. Roy and their mother had still not returned from Berbice. It seemed as though aunt Coreen was sick because their father did not come home at nights until around seven-thirty – and their neighbour said he was at their Cha Cha's.

At about six the neighbour would send Dalip to put on the lights in their house. He always wanted Romesh to be with him because he was scared of the dark, empty house. But if he was afraid of the empty house he was more afraid to tell their neighbour that he was afraid. He was sure she would laugh at him and say that he was foolish. Dalip used to be so scared of the empty house that as soon as he opened the door he would run, hit the switch, run back to the door, push it in and dart down the stairs. When, however, he reached the bottom of the stairs where he knew Romesh and their neighbour could see him, he would walk, pretending to take his time, but he would want to run out of the yard.

Then one day their father decided to take them to the cinema which had recently opened. It was the newest cinema in the country. Another cinema which had been on that very spot had been destroyed by fire. Only once had Dalip been in that cinema. He remembered when they were living in Oliver Street, his Mamoo had taken him there. He remembered that some men riding horses were chasing a train. One man aimed a gun. The muzzle seemed to point straight at him and he screamed. He thought he would be shot, but the gun in the next moment was pointing in another direction. He had not quite recovered from his fright when the train loomed and seemed to rear up suddenly on the screen and head straight for him. He was so scared that he screamed and ducked. His Mamoo put his arm around him and lifted his head from under the chair in front. He explained that it was only a film he was seeing and the train was not real.

A Chinese man who was sitting next to Dalip looked at him and smiled. Dalip felt very foolish and ashamed. He was afraid that everyone would laugh at him when his Mamoo related what had happened. His Mamoo never did and Dalip always respected him for this.

Only on two other occasions Dalip recalled ever going to

a cinema. Both instances occurred when they were living in Oliver Street. The first was when his father took the whole family to see a film called 'Captain Marvel'. In the cinema they went up very high, climbing a long stair. The floor of that part of the cinema sloped down. Dalip was afraid that if he leant forward he would fall into the crowd below. All he seemed to remember of the film was that the 'star-boy' used to say a word like 'Shazaam' and that he could fly. He remembered a lot of noise like thunder in the film. After the show everybody said the film was great. He felt so too except that he did not know why.

He could not remember who took him to the cinema on the next occasion, but he remembered that the film was a western. It had Red-Indians. There was a great battle and one of the Indians seemed to have gotten away. The 'cowboys' these Indians fought, were dressed alike in blue and had big gloves.

When their father had announced that they would be allowed to go to the cinema, Dalip was excited. He had seen the new cinema but had never gone into it. Previously he had always gone to the cinema in the company of some adult. This time, only he and Romesh would be going. Their father said he would give Dalip the money to buy the tickets when he took them to the cinema. Dalip was excited and a bit scared. He had never done this before but he thought he knew what to do.

What was more exciting was that the film they would be seeing would be an Indian film. Dalip had never seen an Indian film. He knew the name of the film was 'Doosti'. He had heard his father singing some of the songs in the bathroom and he had heard some of the songs from this film on the radio. He liked the songs.

It was a Wednesday that Dalip would never forget. When his father took them to the cinema he bought the tickets for Dalip and Romesh, and he bought sweets and nuts for them. Dalip had started to realise that his father was a man who spent money with ease. Dalip liked this. Their father saw them into the cinema. He told them to wait for him after the show as he would be going home from work just after the show ended. That was the first film Dalip saw and understood and remembered from beginning to end. It was a sad film. He felt that he was the hero in the film; that he *would* be the hero. In the film the mother of the 'star' died. His sister disowned him because she had a rich boyfriend. The 'star' had a blind friend who used to beg to get money to see the 'star' through college. The hero was knocked down. His classmates did not like him because of his broken leg which was bandaged and which they said stank, but at the end of the film the 'star-boy' passed his examination and came first in his class and everybody admired him and lifted him on their shoulders when it was announced that he had won a scholarship. Dalip thought he would be as successful as the hero in school and win a scholarship. He felt that the film was especially for him. The film was in Hindi but subtitled in English. Dalip did not know Hindi nor did he know enough English to read the subtitles; yet he understood the film, the whole film. That was something to be happy about.

At the end of the film when they went outside there was a crowd waiting to see the next showing. They waited where their father told them to wait. The long line had almost disappeared and still their father had not come. They were worried. Then Romesh suggested that it was not far to their home, that they walked to and from school everyday and this distance was not much more. Dalip, because he did not want to be outdone by Romesh (he had wanted them to try to get home by themselves but he was not certain they could get home without being lost) readily agreed and said he knew the way home. They held onto each other. They walked in the corner, almost on the grass. They said nothing but walked until they came to the Chinese shop where they bought their groceries each week. They both smiled at each other. They knew their way home from there. They had done something they were proud of.

Later that afternoon they learnt why their father had not come for them as promised. Aunt Coreen had died that afternoon.

Their neighbour told them that their father would not come home till late that night. They would stay with her until he came home. The death seemed to affect everyone, even Romesh, but it had little meaning to Dalip. He did not know why this was so. He barely, in fact, knew that this *was* so. The day had been filled with so many other 'firsts' for him that, though it too was a first, the death was relegated to a relatively unimportant position in his mind. He did not know that then. He did not know that this was the first time he had been related to someone who died and related to the event itself, even though only remotely so.

For some strange reason Romesh went with him later in the evening to put on the lights in their house. He did not know why Romesh volunteered to go with him. He had always gone alone but he was glad to have Romesh there. When he opened the door of the house Romesh held onto his shirt. They hurried to the light switches and hurried out of the house. Dalip was scared but less than usual and he wanted to give Romesh the impression that he was unafraid; he could tell from the way Romesh clutched at the shirt that he was scared.

Later in the evening, when it was almost fully dark, their neighbour noticed that Dalip had not put on the downstairs light; she told him to do so. When Dalip asked Romesh if he would go with him he refused. It was obvious Romesh was scared of something. Dalip had to go alone. He was afraid but he could not bring himself to tell his neighbour or his brother that he was. The bottom of the house was dark and the light switch was in his parents' room. He had hardly ever gone into that room. He opened the door, scooted inside, flung open the bedroom door, hit the switch, ran to the door and closed it. When he looked downstairs the place was dark, the light was not on. Dalip almost wanted to cry and shout in his frustration. He reopened the door and hurried to the bedroom. Something made a noise behind him; he gave a stifled scream and looked around expecting to see something horrible. He saw the door swaying slightly, now and then touching the doorjamb. He saw what he had done. He had put on the bedroom light. He touched the other switch, then took off the bedroom light. He scrambled out of the room and the house. When he stepped onto the platform he was relieved to notice that the downstairs light was on. He closed the door and took his time walking down the stairs. He kept telling himself that he must not be afraid, that there was nothing to be afraid of. The bright light downstairs gave him courage.

Though they tried to sleep they could not. Their neighbour assured them that she would wake them when their father arrived. Dalip and Romesh had a room to themselves; they kept peeping through the glass window expecting their father every minute. Every sound they heard, they imagined to be made by their father but it was always made by something else. When at last he did arrive, they did not know what time it was, nor did they care. What mattered was that he had come home. When their neighbour opened the door to admit him, both boys rushed to him and held on to a leg. He rumpled their hair and spent, it seemed to Dalip, a long time speaking to their neighbour. Dalip did not hear what they said, he did not care. His father was here. He was impatient for them to go home now. He felt so sleepy now. Yet when he and Romesh were on the bed he could not sleep immediately. Their father had enquired if they had liked the film and both boys said that they did. They proceeded in turn, often interrupting each other, to tell their father about the film. They told him proudly that they had walked home from the cinema by themselves without asking anybody for help. He seemed pleased with them. Dalip for the first time in weeks felt happy. While they were talking to their father both of them sat on his lap. They hugged his arm, they played with his fingers. They pulled and admired the hair on his forearm. Dalip noticed that one of his father's fingers had a thicker nail than the others. There was a groove going lengthways on it. He asked his father about it. Romesh examined it. Their father told them that when he was young and used to work in the canefields he had accidentally chopped it with a cutlass.

Dalip had never known that his father used to work in

canefields. He was excited by this new knowledge. Was it before he had married his mother, Romesh asked. Dalip was about to ask the very thing. He told them it was. It seemed strange to Dalip, who always thought he knew about his father, to find out these new things about him. His father mentioned that his Cha Cha had worked there too. Then he seemed to pause.

It was then that Dalip realised that his father had mentioned nothing about his aunt Coreen. Dalip got the impression that his father seemed relaxed, even happy, but not in an obvious way. It seemed to Dalip that it was a long time since he remembered his father being happy.

Now Dalip felt sleepy and he went to bed. Romesh fell asleep almost immediately, before they had said their prayers together, though Dalip had whispered his to himself. The house was dark. Dalip could hear no movement in his parents' room. He thought his father must be asleep. The dark began to frighten him, especially when he suspected he must be the only person awake in the house. He missed Roy now. The bed seemed so empty and large without him. For as long as he could remember, they had always slept on one bed. Whenever Roy was around he never felt scared of anything, because Roy was never scared, except of late of their mother. Dalip buried his face in his pillow to keep from seeing strange shapes in the darkness. He stretched out his hand and touched Romesh. He felt better. He too fell asleep.

The next day, as usual, Romesh and Dalip were under the supervision of their neighbour. The day was sunny. It was windy too but the sun was bright and seemed to bite the flesh. It was about four o'clock when Dalip saw Roy, carrying some bags, enter the gate of their yard. Dalip felt glad, but before he could alert Romesh, he saw his mother. His joy died immediately. The moment she touched the gate she started crying and saying over and over, 'You mean my sister was sick and dying and nobody tell me anything? You mean nobody could tell me, me sister dead even... You mean...' She continued repeating these words until she reached under the house. Their neighbour went across to her.

Dalip was puzzled. He knew that his mother was referring to his aunt Coreen, but why did she call aunt Coreen her sister? They were not sisters, they were not related by blood.

His mother was hardly at home for the next two nights and days, nor was Roy. Roy went with her to his Cha Cha's house, Dalip guessed. Nobody told Dalip and Romesh anything. Whatever they learnt, they overheard from the conversations of the adults around them and they heard more by accident than anything else.

They did not attend the funeral – or rather they were not taken to the funeral. They were not even told of the funeral but they heard about it from the talk around them. Then Roy stayed with them. Some days later, too, their mother stayed at home with them almost all the time. Dalip knew that everything had ended. Dalip got the impression that everything concerning the death of aunt Coreen was deliberately withheld from himself and Romesh. Even Roy, after the funeral, did not speak of the matter at all.

Aunt Coreen had died and was laid to rest. That had no meaning nor made any impression on Dalip. It was something far away, remote, not affecting him.

## Chapter Three

Roy had been a member of the Public Free Library for some time. Their mother insisted that Dalip join too. He would have done so earlier but he had not been old enough. Shortly after his birthday he joined the library. Dalip had not known when his birthday was. One day after he had come home from school his mother called him. He was wondering if he'd done something wrong when she smiled at him, kissed him and said, 'Happy birthday! What would you like? What can mommy give you?' Dalip found it difficult to speak. The way his mother squeezed him and kissed him made him very happy and he had wanted to say that he would have whatever she wished to give him, but he did not want to make a big fuss and let his brothers know.

Dalip felt that his mother liked him more than his other brothers, probably because he was doing very well at school and because one of his teachers had come home and told his mother so. This teacher and his mother were of the same age. What age that was, Dalip could not say exactly, but his mother had looked as if she was about twenty-five years old. Dalip did not find out till much later that his mother and the teacher grew up together. Maybe that was why he sometimes felt he was in love with his teacher.

Before Dalip could say anything his mother announced that she was baking and she would send Roy to purchase ice-cream. There was no ceremony. When the ice-cream was bought everybody shared it.

And when his mother had completed the baking (night was just setting in) they all shared the cakes. Romesh and Dalip could not wait until the cakes cooled. As soon as they were taken out of the oven both Dalip and Romesh wanted them. They got some too. The cakes were hot but delicious, but then Dalip thought that anything his mother baked or cooked was tasty. Almost every Saturday afternoon she baked bread. Whenever she baked, Dalip, Romesh and to a lesser extent, Roy, always hovered around her trying to be helpful; sometimes they would be allowed to grease the baking pans; but they were always waiting for the first set of bread to be finished so that they would get slices – hot slices which they would butter. Dalip liked seeing the butter melt and soak into the bread. One Saturday, Dalip, after buttering his bread, gave his mother a piece. To his surprise and delight she smiled and bit a piece. After that, this became a ritual. He enjoyed giving her a slice of buttered bread, before he ate any. He liked it when sometimes she would be busy and he would put the bread before her mouth and she would bite a piece. He ate the remainder of the slice. After a while Romesh too would do the same thing. Many Saturdays they raced to see who would be the first to butter a piece of bread and offer their mother. Sometimes Romesh would be first. Dalip was always angry on such occasions, and he sometimes felt like telling Romesh not to give their mother bread because he, Dalip, was the one who started the practice. Both Romesh and Dalip were always willing to scrub the pans after baking, but Roy generally did this. They always milled about him, trying to help him.

At first Dalip was frightened by the huge library. The roof was very high. There were books everywhere. But there were also young girls about his age whom he thought looked very pretty and he grew to like going to the library to admire them. He enjoyed searching the shelves for books and borrowing them, especially new ones with large coloured pictures inside. Dalip always had problems selecting a book. Often he would find one only to discover he liked another better five minutes later.

At first, he and Roy went to the library by bus, but after about a month Roy suggested that they walk instead. Dalip did not mind because the buses were always packed with people on

Saturdays, mostly ladies with bags. He did not like being squeezed or having to stand, because when the driver braked, he fell forward or backward into someone. In the crowded bus he could not see outside, but when they walked there were strange houses and unfamiliar streets to see. Walking was always exciting. The first time they walked, Roy did a strange thing.

After they left the library for home, he took Dalip into a huge shop. There was a huge semicircular counter which was shiny and clean. The floor was made of stone, smooth and level; it too was clean and shiny. Around the counter there were round stools fixed into the floor. The stools were made of iron, with soft comfortable tops, but they were high. To get up, Dalip had to climb on the footrest. His feet dangled in the air. The place was crowded but Roy seemed to know what to do. He bought two bottles of drinks – not aerated drinks – some other drink Dalip had never tasted before but which he liked, except that when some got on his hands it was very sticky. Roy also bought various kinds of cakes which were served on small plates which were clean and round. Roy told Dalip that he had used their bus fares to buy these things. He did not have to tell Dalip not to tell their mother. This became a routine every Saturday which Dalip looked forward to eagerly.

There had been bright sunshine early in the morning. It was a Saturday in November. Their mother did not go to work that Saturday, but as usual she got up early and, as was not unusual, she performed puja. Shortly after, their father left for work, their mother left home. She did not tell any of the boys where she was going. Dalip saw her take her bathing suit and put it in a bag. When she left she gave Roy his bus fares to get to the library and return home. She told him to go alone and take Dalip's book with him and return it. Dalip was disappointed.

His mother then left for somewhere. It seemed only a short while before she returned. Roy had just left for the

50

library. Dalip had wondered why she had come back so quickly. He thought that it might have been due to the weather; almost imperceptibly the sun had disappeared. There were black rain clouds above. The rain came down heavily for about half an hour. But that time seemed like a whole day to Dalip. It seemed to him as though the rain had been falling all day and would continue falling for the remainder of the day. Then the dark clouds disappeared and white clouds blanketed out every inch of the blue. The white looked stained and the rain continued, but not as heavily, just heavier than a drizzle. This was starting to irritate Dalip. It meant that he would have to stay indoors, especially with his mother at home. If she were not at home he and Romesh would have run in the rain and splashed in the puddles in the yard. Why did it have to rain that Saturday?

Why did his mother have to be at home that Saturday when it rained? Why did Roy have to go to the library alone? He wondered what Roy was doing. He was getting more irritated the more he thought about everything. Then the rain seemed to pass.

His mother called both Romesh and himself. She did not, she said, feel well – she did not feel like cooking. She gave Romesh money to buy a large tin of sardines and sent him to the shop. She took a letter which was in a sealed envelope and gave it to Dalip. She told Dalip to give the letter to her sister, aunt Sheila, who lived in Oliver Street. She told Dalip not to give the letter to anyone else. Dalip set out in the slight drizzle for Oliver Street. He was glad to be going there. It was a long time since he had been in the street and he was glad that he would be going to his aunt Sheila. Whenever he went to her on any errand for his mother she always spoke nicely to him and always had something nice for him to eat and drink. He liked being in her house. It was small, much smaller than their own but this smallness seemed to make it attractive. There was something in every part of the house; his aunt was very skilled, he thought, at decorating. Her house had so many beautiful ornaments – birds of various kinds; animals; little cars; little

51

toy trucks; statues of people in various dresses and positions. Her house was like a little store.

As he walked through the drizzle with these thoughts in mind he felt pleased with himself. He walked in all the puddles on the road, kicking the water, sometimes walking two or three times through the very large puddles. When he arrived at his aunt's, she told him to wash his feet and go upstairs. She smiled at him.

He hurriedly washed his feet and went upstairs. She gave him a towel to wipe his feet. While he was wiping them he was wondering what good thing his aunt would have for him. He gave her the letter. She told him to sit down. He sat. She tore open the letter and started reading it. Dalip looked at her. She was not as fair as his mother. She was much younger. She was shorter and more fleshy, but not fat. She was very attractive, he thought, but not beautiful, not as beautiful as his mother. He looked at her face... He stopped, surprised. Tears were rolling down her face. She was crying. She stopped, looked at Dalip quickly, tried to brush the tears away and continued reading. Dalip's heart started beating faster. Something was wrong. He had never once seen his aunt cry. She was always pleasant and smiling. Something was wrong he felt, and he was convinced that it had something to do with the letter, with his mother. Suddenly he felt like going home. He did not want to stay any longer. His aunt had stopped crying. Dalip got up. She smiled. She told him to sit. He said he would go. She told him to wait, at least, until the rain stopped falling. He said it was not falling heavily; it was falling only as when he came. He told her he was going and went. When he was on Oliver Street, he turned back. She was standing in the doorway looking after him. He waved. It seemed she hesitated slightly, then she waved back.

Roy and Romesh were sitting downstairs when Dalip arrived home; the house was full of people. He asked Roy what was wrong. He did not answer. Dalip went to the standpipe and washed his feet. There was quite a commotion upstairs. People were constantly entering and leaving the house. All the neighbours around seemed to be present. When he went into the house the furthest he got was the bedroom door of his parents' room. The room was packed with people. Nobody noticed him.

He knew that something was wrong with his mother. Then through the legs of the persons standing in the bedroom doorway he saw something on the ground. It was his mother. His mother on the ground. He could not get in the room and nobody took any notice of him. As he was about to go downstairs he heard someone call his name. He stopped. Somebody from the crowd said to hurry and get his grandmother, his mother's mother. He did not stay to ask any questions. He almost ran all the way to his grandmother who lived about four streets away. When he reached near her house he saw her hurrying out of the yard. She was with a lady. They dashed past him. They did not tell him anything. He felt humiliated. He turned after them. He was exhausted. He could not run anymore. He tried to keep up with his grandmother but she got further and further away from him.

When he returned home, there were two cars in front of the house. Someone said the doctor had arrived. Someone dashed downstairs to phone for the ambulance. There seemed to be more people in the house. More noise was coming from it. He heard his grandmother's voice above all the others. She seemed to be crying or moaning. Roy and Romesh were sitting exactly as he left them, silent and unnoticed. The ambulance arrived. Two men in uniforms went upstairs. Somebody shouted to clear the passage. Roy, Romesh and Dalip got up from the bench downstairs. When they reached the bottom of the stairway they saw the men from the ambulance coming downstairs. They were bearing a stretcher. When they reached abreast of the boys, Dalip saw his mother on the stretcher. Her eyes were closed. He thought she was dead. She was not, but it was the last time Dalip saw his mother alive.

A crowd followed the stretcher out to the ambulance. The boys did not follow them. They went back together silently and sat on the bench under the house.

The house, the yard was deserted except for Roy, Dalip and Romesh who sat downstairs on the bench – waiting. Later from the talk of the adults, Dalip learnt that his mother died just after she reached the hospital.

It was about two o'clock when their father came home. He had been located in the rumshop. Then the boys were noticed. Their mother had taken poison, they learnt. Somebody had thrown the bottle out of the window. Their father and the uncle who was the carpenter looked at it from the window. Why Dalip did it he never knew. He went downstairs and picked up the bottle and held it up to the window above so that his father and uncle could see the bottle better. When his uncle shouted at him he hastily dropped the bottle.

The house started to fill with relatives, some of whom Dalip knew. Two massive tents were put up in the yard, when and by whom Dalip had no idea. But by five o' clock the tents were up. The adults in the house talked incessantly of his mother. Some of them were crying. Nobody seemed to notice Dalip. Roy and Romesh seemed to have disappeared among the relatives. Dalip went on the bridge and sat by himself looking at people going about their business. Then he saw Jim in the distance.

Jim and Dalip and Tony were the best of friends in school. Jim lived in the next street and many Saturdays he would visit Dalip. Sometimes he would ask Dalip's mother for Dalip to go with him to the street corner. His mother used to allow this. Sometimes, as on that particular afternoon, Jim would buy something or bring something with him to eat.

Jim and Dalip would sit on the bridge in the shade and eat whatever Jim brought with him, and talk. They would talk of Tony and school, of books, films, girls, anything which interested them both.

That afternoon Jim brought black pudding. He sat and chatted with Dalip as usual, sharing his black pudding. Then suddenly Jim turned, looked at the house and said laughingly, 'Man, like all-yo' got a wedding or something.' Dalip was disappointed that Jim did not know his mother had died. He

54

expected Jim to know and he expected him to be sympathetic. But he was not.

'My mother dead,' Dalip managed.

'Man, don't make joke,' Jim laughed. Dalip was about to insist but thought best not to. It would seem as though he were begging for sympathy. They laughed and chatted for quite some time. After a time it seemed to Dalip as though nothing unusual had happened. He started telling Jim about the last book he borrowed from the library. It dealt with people living under the sea. It was called the 'Water Babies' or something similar. There were illustrations of water babies in the book. They looked very handsome.

When Jim had gone, Dalip turned from the bridge and looked at the house.

What Jim said seemed true. With the tent and noise issuing from the house it looked as though a celebration was in progress. The presence of so many people in the house gave the impression of some happy event. In the house somebody was cooking, and then Dalip realised that he was hungry and that except for the black pudding he had just shared with Jim, he had not eaten since that morning. Romesh was sitting on the floor in the kitchen. Dalip sat next to him. There was nothing to do but wait until the cooking was finished.

This seemed to go on for almost a week. It appeared as though the funeral was being delayed because of Dalip's two Mamoos, both of whom were working far away in the Interior. During that time Dalip did not go to school. In fact, for the remainder of the term, one month, Dalip did not attend school nor Romesh, though Roy did. Each night the pattern seemed to be the same. Women upstairs, men downstairs. Singing of *bhajans* and crying upstairs; rum-drinking, laughter, dominoes, cards downstairs. During the day more and more relatives came to meet and sympathise with Dalip's father. It seemed to Dalip that everyday some relative or friend whom Dalip's father had not seen for ages, came from a different part of the country to sympathise with him.

Then one day Dalip's Mamoo, who was working in the

Interior, came to town. He was the eldest of Dalip's Mamoos. The youngest one, also working in the Interior could not be located. The eldest Mamoo said when he heard the message he had sent to his brother's 'base-camp' but his brother was not there. He had left a message.

On the day of the funeral the yard overflowed with people. Dalip saw some of his teachers and classmates. His classmates were noticeable in their uniforms. Teachers and students from Roy's school were also present. Margaret Street could not hold all the cars. Some had to be parked in the avenue and even the two other streets nearby.

The moment the hearse arrived there was a wail from the women. The coffin was brought into the yard and placed under the house. People in a constant stream kept looking in.

Roy and Romesh and Dalip were kept near the coffin. Everybody kept telling them many things which Dalip could not remember. He could not understand what everyone was making such a fuss about. He did not see it as important, being near the coffin, but he and Roy and Romesh were patted and told so many tender things that Dalip felt he was obliged to stay close. If he had moved from there he would have been lost in the crowd.

Then it was decided to take the coffin upstairs. There were problems getting it up the stairs, then it seemed that it would not pass through the doorway. Dalip heard somebody say, 'Savitri, girl, why are you making so much problems? Make things easier for us. Please Savitri, behave yourself.' Almost immediately it seemed, to Dalip, the coffin of its own volition went into the house. There were no problems with the coffin after that. In the hall where the coffin was placed, Dalip noticed Roy crying. He did not expect that from Roy. Roy had always seemed so sure and confident of himself. He thought Roy was foolish to cry. He could not understand his crying. Almost every person upstairs was crying – male and female. Dalip could not understand this. All this seemed senseless to him. It was something one might expect from women. It meant nothing to him. What if somebody dies? What did it matter? He would show them it did not matter. He did not cry. He saw no reason for it. Even Romesh was sobbing. For what, Dalip had no idea.

The car provided by the funeral parlour for the relatives of the deceased was occupied by Romesh, Roy and Dalip and their eldest Mamoo. His father and his Cha Cha and his carpenter uncle travelled together in another car. The procession moved very slowly. Whenever Dalip looked back, the line of cars stretched as far as his eyes could see.

At last they reached the burial ground. The coffin was placed on the ground and the pandit read some mantras. Dalip's father, Roy, Dalip and Romesh had to go round the coffin a number of times under the instruction of the pandit. Then his father rubbed something red down the forehead of his mother. The coffin was closed and put in the tomb. Earth was thrown after the coffin. Dalip did not know why but he too threw mud because everybody seemed to be doing so and because somebody said to do so. The tomb was closed to wailing from Dalip's aunts.

That night was little different from any other of the past week. The next day seemed to be the same, and the next. Then there was a change. Dalip's cousins, his Cha Cha's sons, came to stay with them. Dalip guessed that school must have closed for the Christmas holidays. Now everything was livelier with his cousins around. The boys always found some mischief or something exciting to do. They experimented with the 'fireside' which was set up downstairs. Because of the large number of people present it was found more convenient to cook meals downstairs. The boys had heard about roasting plantains in the simmering embers and decided to try it. First they had to smuggle plantains from the kitchen upstairs, then put them in the ashes. They had to linger round the fireside seemingly casually, turn the plantains to prevent them from being burnt, all without being observed. One plantain was taken out and sampled. It was tasty. All the others were taken out, peeled and distributed. This became a daily ritual. The more they did, the less they cared about being seen. They tried sweet potatoes and eddoes. Nobody seemed to bother them. At night they all slept together on the floor on jute bags on which sheets were spread.

There seemed to be lots of rum-drinking by the men. The rum bottles piled up. The boys stole some 'empties' whenever they could and sold them. The money they got was used to buy sweets and a variety of other things. The whole holidays seemed to be spent like this. Games were played – hide-and-seek, war games, sometimes cards, snakes and ladders, ludo, monopoly. All the boys enjoyed themselves thoroughly. It was all that mattered. They told each other stories and jokes and they overheard stories and jokes from the men which were not meant for their ears. These were wicked jokes. He remembered the one with the two parrots. According to the tale, a man had two parrots. One with white feathers and one with green feathers. The one with white feathers was a 'cussing' parrot – it only knew how to scream foul language while the one with green feathers knew how to preach. One day a priest who was passing heard the 'preaching' parrot and thought it would be good for his congregation. He expressed his desire to buy the parrot from the owner. The owner agreed and told the priest to return the next day. When the priest had gone, the owner set to work painting the parrots. He painted the green one white and the white one green. The next day, Sunday, when the preacher came, he was sold the white parrot, painted green. The owner advised him to pull the tail of the parrot when he wanted it to speak.

Later that Sunday morning, facing his congregation, the preacher cleared his throat, 'Ladies and gentlemen,' he said, 'this morning, by the grace of our Lord Jesus Christ I have a surprise for you. A miracle some would say, but in reality the wonderful work of our Lord God. We have with us a preaching parrot which will give this morning's sermon. Without further ado I hand you over to this Godly parrot.' At this point, as instructed, the pastor pulled the tail of the parrot, which reared and screamed, 'Why the cunt are you pulling my tail?' The preacher, outraged, stammered, 'What, what you said?'

'Why the cunt you pull my tail? You deaf you ass don't hear?' the parrot replied. The pastor, outraged, picked up the collection plate and flung it at the parrot. The parrot ducked, the plate barely missing its head. Then it said:

'Man you playing Ajab nuh. Man, if ah didn't duck you woulda fuck off meh head.' The story ended there with peels of laughter.

There were countless others which Dalip found amusing. These and the games helped to make the holidays very interesting. It did not seem to Dalip that there had been a death. But then the holidays ended. It was time for his cousins to return home. It was time for Dalip to return to school.

# Chapter Four

Two days before school reopened, before the end of the Christ-mas holidays, a Saturday, Dalip's father, his Cha Cha and his uncle who was the carpenter (the boys now called him uncle Ruddy) were downstairs under the house. It was about ten o'clock. They had spread jute bags on the concrete and were seated on them. They were drinking rum and talking. Dalip, who was feeling desolate because his cousins had just been sent home by his Cha Cha, fastened himself to his father. It was then he was first conscious of missing his mother. He knew that if she had been around he would not have dared be anywhere close to his father once he was drinking rum and gaffing with friends and relatives.

They were interrupted by a cycle bell. The postman was standing at the gate. Before anyone could tell Dalip to collect the mail, he was already at the gate. He collected an envelope from the postman. It was for his father; it was larger than a normal envelope, as large as a book. He ran with the envelope to his father who took it. As his father tore the edge, Dalip held onto his arm hoping to see what was in the envelope. There were photographs. Photographs of his mother. Sud-denly all the photographs fell from his father's fingers and he started to sob like a child. Dalip could not understand why his father should cry because he saw photographs of his mother. Dalip felt uncomfortable and as an excuse to move away from his father he bent and picked up the photographs.

He saw his mother seated on the floor of some room. It looked like the floor of the photo-studio where his father had once brought them all to have a photograph taken. His mother seemed to stare straight at him. There was a slight smile on her face, but something sad too. One moment he saw a smile and the next, sadness. Then he saw both together.

His father was still sobbing. His face was hidden in his hands. Instinctively Dalip turned and gave the photographs to his Cha Cha and he went and stood next to him as he examined them. There were three in all. The photographs were similar in size and in black and white. His mother had on her bathing suit. She looked very beautiful. Dalip had thought she looked like a film star. His Cha Cha turned the photographs around. There were stamp marks at the back of all the photographs. Stamp marks with dates. His Cha Cha seemed to shiver for a moment. Speechless he passed one of the photographs to uncle Ruddy who looked at the photograph for a long time then turned it around and looked at the back. It seemed as though somebody had slapped him. He jerked his face, looked at Dalip's Cha Cha and said,      'This   tek out the day Savitri died!'

'Tha' is just wha' I realise,' Dalip's Cha Cha said.

'I know now. Now I know!' Dalip exclaimed before he could stop himself.

'Know wha'?' his Cha Cha and uncle Ruddy asked together. Dalip hesitated. He had not meant to say anything.

'On the morning mommy died she went out with her bathing suit. She didn't stay long. I di' think that was because of de rain she come back so quick and didn't go an' swim.'

'What else she do, when she come home?'

Dalip felt scared; his Cha Cha spoke harshly. 'She sent Romesh at the shop to buy sardine and she sent me to auntie Sheila with a letter.

'What!' Dalip's Cha Cha and uncle Ruddy looked at each other.

'What letter? What the letter had inside?' Dalip's father asked softly.

Dalip had forgotten about him. 'I ... I don't know; the letter was sealed and mommy said not to give anybody except auntie Sheila.'

'You take the letter to her? You give she it?'

'Yes.'

'You give it to Sheila?'

'Yes.'

'Was anybody else home?'

'No.' Everyone seemed to be asking questions. There were anxious looks on all the faces. Dalip knew that they would ask more questions. These questions made him jittery. There was only one way to stop the questions and that was to tell them all he knew.

'When I gave she the letter, she tear it and read it. Then she start to cry. When she see me looking at she, she wipe she eyes and tell me wait till the rain done. But I didn't wait. I walk through the rain and come home. When I reach home, Romesh and Roy did sitting down on the bench, down de.' Dalip pointed to the bench not far from them, and continued, 'A lot a people pass upstairs. I want to go in the room, but I couldn't pass, but I see mommy on the ground. Then somebody sen' me to call granny. I run all the way, but when I reach near, she and a lady come out the yard walking fast. When I reach back home the house had more people.    It    had two cars outside and somebody say the doctor come. Then the ambulance come. The ambulance man tek mommy away on a stretcher. Then everybody go away. Nobody tell we anything.

Dalip's father had started crying again. His Cha Cha and uncle Ruddy started to tell him to 'take things easy' and other calming words. They did not notice Dalip slip away.

School reopened. Dalip was in the second standard then. He was a curiosity in school. For the first two weeks everybody seemed to want to speak to him, but they hardly did. Gradually the boys started to treat him as though nothing had happened. Then one day somebody asked him about his mother. He did not hear exactly what was asked but he knew it was about his mother. He dreaded the question; he found himself stifled, he could not speak. He made a conscious effort but words did not come. He stared around at the expectant faces hopelessly. He tried to explain that he was trying to but still the words would not come. Then Jim came to his rescue; he told them not to bother Dalip. Dalip was silently grateful.

One midday as Dalip was going home for lunch, a girl who was in standard four asked him how his mother died. Dalip had seen the girl often. She lived in the next street and often walked the same way as Dalip. There was silence after the question. They were on the street walking. Dalip felt that he could not answer. He felt sad. He felt as though he would suffocate. The girl asked again. He looked at her, speechless. He felt something building up inside. He turned from the girl who was looking at him. He looked at the ground, at the pebbles on the road. He saw the pebbles change shape. He knew tears were in his eyes. He tried to hold them back. There was the girl beside him. He was faintly conscious that there were many students in front of him and behind him. Tears flowed down his face. He started to cry on the road as he continued walking towards his home. The girl slowed down. He was vaguely aware that a group of girls caught up with her. He did not slacken or quicken his pace. He continued walking.

Afterwards, any time anybody asked him about his mother he would cry. On each occasion he tried to stop himself but he could not. Each time he heard the dreaded question he would try with all his energy not to begin to cry but he would. Sometimes while walking home after school other students would make remarks about him and his mother. Immediately he would feel the tears in his eyes. Dalip got the impression that one or two of the boys would deliberately ask him about his mother, to see if it was true that he would cry when asked the question. Word seemed to have gotten around the whole school.

Gradually, though, the questioning ended. School started to become bearable. There was a new admission to his class, a girl with short hair which curled inwards. There was no doubt she was beautiful; they all thought so, but nobody got along with her. She hardly spoke to anybody. She was rude, Dalip felt, quick to speak harshly when anybody spoke to her.

They started to call her a 'pepper-fly'. It was made worse by the fact that every morning her father brought her to school in a car, the only parent who did so, though other parents had cars. The more the boys spoke of her among themselves, and the more they avoided her, the more Dalip felt he must speak to her if only to belittle her.

One day he told Jim and some other boys he would speak to her. They laughed at him and said he must be joking. They dared him to call her 'pepper-fly'. At that moment, Salima entered the class. Without thinking Dalip walked up to her, called her 'pepper-fly' and told her some other things which he had not thought of before, nor could remember afterwards, but they were harsh things. Then he left her, speechless, without waiting for her to say anything and walked back to the boys who were laughing. After that she spoke more often to the girls and less harshly. The boys addressed her more frequently too but she was still at times harsh with them. She was never harsh with Dalip, but then Dalip rarely spoke to her. He would look at her when no one was looking. Sometimes their eyes would meet but only fleetingly. Dalip would look away immediately, giving her the impression that it was just by chance he had looked in her direction. But the boys and girls noticed that she was never harsh with Dalip and the boys used to call Dalip, Salima, and tease him about her. At first they did this only among themselves but later they did this when the others were present and occasionally when Salima was present. Actually Dalip felt he was in love with Salima, but he was afraid to speak to her. He gave her the impression that he was still as harsh with her. Sometimes he wanted to tell the boys not to tease him about Salima when she was near; he sensed that she did not like this but he knew that if he did this the boys would deliberately tease him in front of her.

Salima and Dalip were soon separated, however. In that very term, shortly after her arrival, (it was only about three weeks after school reopened) Dalip, Jim and Tony were removed from the second standard. The teachers thought them to be academically the best students in their year. They were allowed to move over to the 'Common Entrance' class where they would be writing the examination which, if passed, would give them the chance of five years free secondary education. Dalip did not have time to think about Salima now. The teachers gave the students in this class a lot of work, a lot of homework too.

When Dalip told his father what had happened he seemed indifferent. Dalip was hurt. He missed his mother then. She would have been overjoyed. She would have hugged him and kissed him. She would have made him feel that he had accomplished something. She would have sent for ice-cream or baked cakes. But Dalip worked, nevertheless. He hoped to perform well enough to pass the 'Common Entrance' examination with the best of marks and to be admitted to no other school but the best in the country, the revered Queen's College – that would have been what his mother would have wanted; *that*, Dalip was sure, would impress his father. Apart from this he worked with extra zeal because the competition in the class was keen and he wanted to do better than everybody else. Like the star-boy in the Indian film he had seen, 'Doosti', he wanted to top his whole class.

Almost every afternoon, Dalip, Jim and Tony, with some others, had to remain in school for extra lessons. Their teacher told them that they had to catch-up with the others. None of them minded. They had their fun from extra lessons too, or rather more, from *after* extra lessons. School was dismissed at three o'clock, but lessons would last until forty-five minutes past three.

The fifteen minutes until four the boys spent playing. They knew that their parents stopped work at four o'clock and did not usually reach home until about half-past four. They played many games, but the favourite was floating bits of wood in a nearby canal. Recently a huge pipe had been installed in this canal to help the flow of water into a larger canal. The water always raced through this pipe. One boy, stooped slightly, could fit comfortably in the pipe, which was long like a tunnel. The boys would get pieces of sticks, leaves, paper (sometimes they would make paper boats) and drop whatever it was in the water at one end of the pipe, then race to the other and wait to see whose boat would come out first. They would count whose boat came out first the most times and kept a tally of who won every afternoon. Because the winner varied, the boys were never tired of this game. Often they would spend more than the fifteen minutes, forgetting about time in their excitement. In addition to this, sometimes lessons lasted longer than usual and the boys were later home. Jim did not have to worry; his father always believed that he was late because of the lessons, but Tony said they should be careful because his father did not like him to be home later than four o'clock. Dalip had no problem. His father, now that his mother was no longer around, rarely came home early.

One afternoon, lessons finished late. There was sun. For the past week it had rained almost every afternoon. The boys had not had a chance to sail their boats. That afternoon they were overjoyed because of the sun and because the recent rains had made the water level rise and caused the water to flow so fast through the pipe there was froth at one end of it. That afternoon, when they dropped their boats, almost as soon as they reached the other end their boats came out. The cycle continued over and over: they dropped their boats, raced to the other end to ascertain the winner, went back, got fresh bits of sticks, paper, bits of fallen tree limbs; they laughed, they kept their tallies. The boats came through the pipe very close together sometimes. Sometimes there were mild disputes as to whose came first, but these were good-natured. They forgot about time. Dalip noticed a man on a cycle across the road, in the corner, watching them, but the excitement made him forget the man until Jim noticed him too. He stooped. He whispered to Tony that his father was watching them. Tony stopped. Dalip saw the fear on his face. The man started to move towards the boys. Dalip did not know what to do. He wanted to hide but could not move. He was afraid for Tony and himself, afraid that the man would whip not only Tony but himself too. Tony's father reached them. He scrambled Tony by his ear, he looked harshly at Jim and Dalip and ordered them home. They did not wait. Dalip had an overwhelming urge to urinate. When he glanced back he saw Tony receive a few slaps. Dalip walked faster. He glanced back again and saw Tony being towed by his father on the next street. They did not linger and play anymore after lessons.

One day Dalip's teacher told him to tell his father that he should come into school and bring along Dalip's birth certificate. Dalip passed on the message; his father seemed displeased. He did not go. The next week the teacher told him again to ask his father to come. Again he told his father, who muttered something about having to get time off from work. The teacher asked Dalip that afternoon whether he had told his father and Dalip told him he had. The teacher did not ask him again. About two weeks later his teacher told him that he could not write his 'Common Entrance' examination that year, perhaps next, but not that year, though he could continue in the common entrance class. Dalip wanted to cry. His teacher explained that it was because his father had not filled in the necessary forms or sent Dalip's birth certificate. When the boys in the class learnt of this they felt sorry for Dalip. He did not feel like working anymore. He went through the motions but without any enthusiasm. Often, when they had reading sessions, he would have his book open and be looking intently at it, but he saw nothing most of the time but images of himself with his teacher who was naked, on the floor, on a bed and one time in a tree.

Dalip renewed his acquaintance with the boys in the second standard. He did not see much of Jim and Tony except in the form room. Now he smiled at Salima. She smiled at him.

Shortly afterwards they began exchanging words, but this was only possible when she came to school early, which was a rarity; her father tended to deliver her to school only just before the bell was rung. On the occasions when she came early he learnt from her where she lived, that her father had a business. He did not know exactly what it was, but it sounded

67

important. He learnt too that she walked home with her sister in the afternoons after school. He asked if he could walk with her. She said yes, but not all the way home because her father might see her from his store. She also cautioned him that when he walked with her he should not say anything because her sister would tell her father everything. He also had to make it appear as though he had to walk in the same direction as the girls to get to his home. It was in fact the opposite direction to Dalip's home, but he did not mind. Many afternoons he would walk silently with Salima and her sister. At the junction of the street where Salima lived Dalip would walk north to the next corner while Salima would turn east. At first Dalip liked walking silently with Salima but as the weeks wore on he became increasingly irritated with this silence. He could not bear it; he spoke to her one afternoon.

The next day Salima told him that he could not walk with her anymore because her sister had told her father. Dalip still persisted, but he would not walk beside Salima anymore, but just a little behind. She scarcely noticed him, but when she glanced at him she always appeared angry. After about a week of this he stopped. He could not bear her angry looks, and he too started to feel angry, and irritated and frustrated. He wanted to make her feel as he was feeling.

Then sometime in May, just before the annual examin-ations, the school held a fair. There had been lots of prep-arations for it and his anticipation grew as it neared the Saturday afternoon when it opened. At the fair there was a pole with hundreds of ribbons, each held by a beautiful little girl. They pranced between each other in a circle round the pole as the ribbons got shorter. When the girls had finished everybody clapped, including Dalip. It had been splendid. Then the crowd began to disperse to various parts of the school grounds. Dalip saw Salima in the crowd. His heart raced as he tried to get her attention. He could not, and as he tried to walk through the bodies to get near her, she disappeared. He started searching for her, bumping into some of the boys from the second standard. They seemed excited and closed around him, telling him that they had been looking for him. Salima was upstairs; she was going with her chit to collect her ice-cream and cakes. They all raced upstairs. Salima was near the ice-cream stand talking to some girls. Dalip went up to them, not knowing what to do. The other boys hung back. When the girls noticed Dalip they parted and moved to one side. Dalip smiled, but Salima stared coldly at him. He called her name but she did not answer. The boys behind him started to laugh. Dalip was furious. He snatched the ice-cream chit out of her hand and turned round, showing it to the boys. They flocked round him now, laughing at Salima. Dalip had meant to tease her and then give her back the chit, but he found himself wanting to hurt her first, as she had hurt him. He offered her the chit, but when she stretched out her hand he pulled it back. Before he knew what was happening, Salima burst into tears. Everybody turned on Dalip accusingly – even the boys. He felt guilty and ashamed – and afraid. What if some teacher came up now and found out what he had done? Some of the boys told him to run and hide by the washstand before any teacher came. He bolted downstairs.

There were huge posts by the washstands. Dalip hid himself behind one and waited. His heart seemed to grow larger, as if it would burst. Each minute he expected to see some teacher with a cane in his hand come hunting for him. When the boys found him Dalip asked them anxiously what had happened. They told him that Salima had stopped crying and they had gotten her ice-cream for her, but she had said she would tell her father what he had done. Dalip felt there would be trouble; his friends agreed. What would he do if Salima's father came in school after him on Monday morning? Then somebody came up with a plan. If on Monday morning when Salima came to school, her father got out of the car, the boys would position themselves by the gate at the north, they would signal to Dalip who would be by the south end of the building. He would then hide by the washstands.

Dalip had a horrid Sunday. He feared that Salima's father would trash him and, worse, tell his father. Dalip knew that would mean a sound thrashing with his father's broad leather belt if he found out about the incident.

On Monday morning Dalip did not want to go to school, but he could find no excuse to stay away, yet in a sense he wanted to go. Whatever had to happen he wanted it to happen and be done with quickly. The boys were waiting for him, positioned as planned. Dalip's heart hit against his chest. He wanted to scream and cry his fear out, but he could not do that. Then he saw the blue car belonging to Salima's father. He hid himself behind a post. Her father came out. Only Salima had come to school that day. He said something to Salima and followed her into the school yard. The boys waved frantically. Dalip pulled in and sneaked off to the washstands. He waited. Then the boys appeared, smiling. Salima's father was gone.

It was around the time of the incident with Salima that Dalip started to have nightmares. He was sleeping at this time with his father. Roy and Romesh, who had a bed to themselves, at first used to tease him and tell him that he was sleeping on the bed on which their mother died, on the very side she used to sleep. Dalip had not taken this seriously, but of late he had begun to wonder. Sometimes he felt scared, but only fleetingly, for whenever he woke up, his father was always present, and even if his father was asleep, he would feel reassured and comforted and go back to sleep. Then a strange thing started to happen. Several mornings, when he woke, his father would ask him about a black fowl, would ask him where the black fowl was buried. Dalip was puzzled and could not answer. But as almost every morning his father asked him the same question, he decided to clear the matter up once and for all. The next time his father asked about the black fowl he found enough courage to ask his father what he was talking about. His father was silent for some time. Then he explained. Many times, his father told him, he would toss and turn in his sleep and mumble about some black fowl being buried somewhere and that in his sleep he always declared that he had to find this fowl. That was strange, Dalip told his father, he couldn't recall ever dreaming about a black fowl. When his

70

father had gone to work, Roy confirmed what his father had said, that many nights he too had heard Dalip mumbling about some black fowl. Dalip promised himself that he would try to remember his dreams.

After that, he did not seem to be getting this dream anymore. Then another strange thing happened. He overheard his father telling his Cha Cha and uncle Ruddy that he was having nightmares fairly often and in these nightmares he dreamt of Dalip's mother. He explained to his brother and uncle Ruddy that Dalip's mother always kept telling him that she wanted Dalip with her. He said that this happened often and he was especially worried because, as he told them, in Dalip's dreams of the black fowl, and in his talking at nights he had often mentioned his mother. Dalip was shocked. His father had never told him that he mentioned his mother in connection with his dreams. Dalip heard uncle Ruddy tell his father to 'tie down the house'. Dalip did not know what that meant. His Cha Cha said that this should be done as a last resort if the unusual dreams did not stop. Then Dalip started to feel that if the house was 'tied down' his nightmares would stop, as would his father's.

Dalip's father seemed to spend more and more time out of the house. He would get up early in the morning and prepare lunch. For breakfast they usually had biscuits or bread, the midday meal usually rice and curry or stew. In the afternoons the boys had to cook. They made roti and curried, stewed or fried vegetables or greens. They frequently roasted *bhaigan* then peeled off the skin and prepared it. Years later, when they were in their teens, they learnt that *bhaigan* was what the other world, the world not consisting of East Indians, called the egg plant. Actually Roy did the cooking, but in time both Romesh and Dalip learnt. They learnt to make roti – the mixing of the flour, *belaying* it into circular discs, baking these discs on the *thawa*, and then cooking them over the naked flame. Then the brothers could take spells cooking, though Roy cooked most of the time with Dalip and Romesh in

71

attendance.

They divided the housework too. While the roti and curry or stew were being cooked, one person would sweep the kitchen and wipe the shelves. Another would wash all the dishes. Sometimes they rotated the tasks. They were always careful not to burn the roti since their father would scold them if it was burnt. They made sure that if this ever happened they disposed of any burnt roti, by eating them of course. They had more than enough time to do this because their father rarely came home before eight o'clock, having at lunch time issued instructions as to what had to be done and what was to be cooked in the afternoon.

Dalip had often to go to bed before his father arrived home. As soon as Dalip and Romesh were in bed and he had finished dropping the mosquito nets, Roy would turn off the light and go to bed himself. It was at these times that Dalip remembered his brothers' teasings and the things he had heard his father speaking of. One night he lay in bed; Romesh was dropping the net in the other bedroom and he could hear Roy asking him if he was finished and Romesh saying that he would be in a minute. Dalip anticipated the moment when the lights would be put out. Then Romesh said that he was finished. The lights went out. He heard Roy walking in the next bedroom and then he thought he heard him getting into bed. Then he heard something else. Someone seemed to push open the door to his bedroom. He heard the sound distinctly. Lying on his back, looking at the roof, he could not turn or move. Then the person – he was convinced it was someone – stepped onto the bed. The springs of the mattress creaked. There were one, two, three steps. Then the person stepped over him. He felt the air as the foot moved over him and the person seemed to walk through the window. Dalip screamed. In a flash the light was on and Roy was in the room asking what had happened. Dalip could not speak for a while. All the brothers gathered outside in the hall. When Dalip could speak he hesitated; he knew that his brothers would not believe and that Roy might laugh at him. Dalip was convinced it was not his imagination.

He had heard many persons say that there were no such things as spirits and that persons who claimed to see spirits really saw nothing but what they imagined. Dalip had never till then believed in spirits, but he was convinced someone had walked over him. Someone from another world, someone not living. He should have seen the outline of the body but saw nothing. When he finally told them his experience he told it with such conviction that Roy did not laugh at him. Roy told him to sleep with them in the next room until their father came home. But he did not. They talked for some time then they all went to bed again. Roy, at Dalip's request, left one light on.

That night he had nightmares. In his first nightmare he saw his mother in a coffin, but the coffin was flat on the floor in front of the bathroom and it seemed as though his mother wanted limes.

When he woke up terrified, he saw his father asleep on the bed. He did not know when his father had come in. All the lights were off. Dalip sat up in the bed for some time, then he went back to sleep touching his father's arm for reassurance. Later that night he dreamt of his mother again and for the first time he remembered the dream. He must have spoken in his sleep because the next morning his father asked him about the black fowl. He told him that his mother had appeared in his dream telling him about the black fowl. She had been trying to speak, her mouth had formed the words. He thought she had said 'backstep' but could not be certain.

Often this dream recurred. Then – it was just after the school closed for the August vacation – he became certain of what his mother said. This time when she opened her mouth he heard the words clearly. She told him the black fowl was buried near the corner post of the house, the front corner post, the one to the north-east. He told his father.

Two weeks of the holiday had passed when one morning he found his father and brothers watching over him waiting for him to wake. His father asked him if he remembered what had happened during the night.

He could not; he had had a normal night's rest. This

happened on a further two mornings. He felt that his father and Roy looked at him as though he were some strange creature. When Dalip asked Roy what happened in the night, Roy would not tell him. Dalip believed that Roy had been instructed to say nothing to him. The next morning uncle Ruddy slept with Roy and Romesh. In the morning he too looked at Dalip curiously and asked if he remembered what had happened during the night, but he could not and said so. Uncle Ruddy was baffled. Dalip's aunts and Mamoo came to see him during the course of the week. They all asked questions he could not remember and everybody treated him as though he was a creature from another planet.

It was suggested that he be taken to spend his holidays on the East Bank of the Demerara river with his Nana – his mother's father. Dalip was glad. He would be with his mother's stepbrothers again. He liked them and he liked being there. He remembered all the pleasant things he had done and experienced on his first holiday there. Dalip was surprised when he reached his grandfather's house. The old house had gone, the site built over. In its place was a much larger house, much larger than the old one. It was painted nicely. There were many large rooms in this house and the roof was high and this made the bedrooms appear very spacious. Dalip was given a small bed all to himself, but he slept in a room with his eldest uncle, the one who had taken him to the Christian churches and who always seemed kind and gentle. His two elder uncles were working, so Dalip spent most of his time with his grandfather. He went with him everywhere. He liked going into the compound of the mandir during the day, especially in the mornings. The pandit who lived in a building behind the mandir always seemed to have some business with his grandfather, sometimes with other persons. Dalip was the only boy around and he would be left to roam the compound.

It was filled with flowering trees of all shapes and colour, neat beds with flower plants. Dalip loved roaming among them. He followed the numerous butterflies. He looked at lizards and ants. He felt happy and contented. He used to think that paradise must be just as beautiful as those sunny mornings when he had the freedom of the mandir yard, when he wandered between the plants at will, following butterflies and birds and lizards, hearing the whistling of the birds and the wind in the trees, yet sensing a deep and calming silence at the same time.

One morning though, everyone was crowded around him when he woke up. They asked him if he remembered what he did. He shook his head and asked them to tell him. One of his uncles looked at him with wide eyes and open mouth.

'What you did? What you did? Last night about ten times you fly up in the air and knock the roof. If I didn't see it myself I could never believe it.' Dalip glanced up at the roof in disbelief. It was very, very high; he could not in his wildest dreams touch that roof by himself, unaided, by jumping in the air from the bed. Then he knew why his father and Roy and uncle Ruddy had looked at him so strangely. During the next week something similar happened twice. Dalip, though, never remembered anything of the events described to him afterwards.

He remembered his grandfather taking him to the mandir. His grandfather went inside and stayed a long time with the pandit. Then they called Dalip into the building. A big book was open in front of the pandit. He made some motion over Dalip with his hand and told him to sit. He then read something from the book. It seemed to last for some minutes. Dalip thought the pandit was reading in Hindi, but he was not sure. The words sounded like Hindi words. Dalip was sent outside. Shortly after his grandfather came out of the building. From that day nothing had ever happened to Dalip or bothered him. The nightmare of the black fowl and his mother ceased and he did not jump to touch the roof anymore.

# Chapter Five

When the next death occurred Dalip was in the fourth form. It was a Sunday, the day before the first subjects of the end-of-year examinations would be written. Dalip had just come out of the bathroom, a towel wrapped round his waist, when one of his cousins arrived. He thought that his cousin had come visiting, as he did sometimes, but he announced without any introduction, 'Daddy's dead.' Dalip thought his cousin was joking, but the cousin asked for Dalip's father, who was resting. When he heard the news he said nothing. He went into his room, put on some clothing and left the house with his nephew, leaving Dalip at home. His Cha Cha was dead; Dalip felt it could not be real.

He heard the ticking of a three-speed bicycle as he was dressing. He knew it was Roy, who had only recently bought a bicycle, a lady's cycle with nickel fender and nickel carrier. It was second hand, but it looked like a new bicycle because Roy had it glittering all over. Every Sunday afternoon he would wash and polish the cycle, bathe, then go for a ride on the seawall or in the gardens, to meet some girl or other, Dalip suspected. Roy was popular with girls; he whistled pleasantly and well – he did everything pleasantly and well. He almost always smiled and laughed.

When he came into the bedroom, Dalip was combing his hair.

'Going out?' Roy asked.

'Joking? Exams begin tomorrow,' Dalip replied, half-seriously. Roy sat on the edge of the bed. Dalip looked at him reflected in the mirror. Who would have believed; it seemed only the other day that they were little boys and their mother was dead. He remembered then. 'Cha Cha died this afternoon. We just learnt. Daddy left at once.' Dalip looked in the mirror at Roy for a reaction. Roy, who was bending to take off a sock, straightened.

'How?' Their eyes locked in the mirror.

'Don't know yet...'

'Better get some sleep,' he said, 'Wake me up around seven.' There was a pause, then he added, 'You look tense. A walk or ride would be good for you. It might help to relax you.' Dalip left the room, thinking about what Roy had said. He got along easily with Roy, yet felt he was someone to respect. Whenever Roy said something he always had good reason and he was usually correct. Dalip collected his bicycle. It was actually his mother's cycle which Roy had been using before he bought his own. He rode out to the seaside and sat on the wall. As usual there were other people on the seawall, including a number of girls, but that afternoon he did not bother much with them. He was thinking about the last death among his relatives. That was when his mother had died. So many things had changed. So many persons had changed. In particular he thought about Roy and how important he had become to him.

After his mother died, his father had not seemed to care about them or what they did. Roy left school the next year. He had wanted to go on to Secondary school, but he was afraid to ask his father to allow him to do so, to pay the school fees each term. His father had become very snappy about money matters. Dalip too was always afraid to ask his father for money to buy exercise books or text books. Roy had drifted from one odd job to another until he found a job as a handyman in one of the large department stores in the city. As Dalip sat on the seawall he thought of how much Roy had changed. The fact was that he was going to secondary school now *because* of Roy. Roy had volunteered to pay the school fees for Dalip even though he was only earning a small wage. His father helped only after Roy took it upon himself to see that Dalip went to a secondary school. The only other time Dalip's father helped was at the beginning of each school year when he bought all the books that were on the list attached to the school report. If Dalip needed any books during the term, his father's grumbling that things were 'hard' made Dalip refrain from asking him. He would instead ask Roy, who if he did not have money at the time, would tell Dalip to wait until the end of that week or the end of the next week when he got his wages. The only other thing Dalip's father helped with was providing Dalip with two school shirts and a school pants each school year. Sometimes he provided him with shoes, but most of the clothing that Dalip wore was either clothing which had become too tight for Roy, or clothing which Roy bought for him. Roy dressed well and was very good looking. He was around twenty years old, Dalip thought, about four or five years older than himself, but he did not know for certain.

When Dalip returned home he woke Roy; it was nearly seven. Roy had a bath, ate and set out for his Cha Cha's house. For the next three nights both Roy and his father came home late. Dalip had wanted to attend the wake but because of his examinations he could not. He wanted to attend the funeral, but that very afternoon he had a Geography exam. So like the death of his mother and the death of his aunt Coreen, this death could mean little to him.

The week after the funeral, Dalip was still revising; he had one more subject to take before completing his examinations. Roy was in the room reading a novel. They both looked up at the same time. There was a strong smell of cigarette smoke. Their father was not at home and the smell was a peculiar one, the peculiar flavour noticeable when their Cha Cha smoked. This incident never recurred.

When Dalip went into the fifth form, the year passed quickly. He studied hard, he wanted to excel, he wanted to go on to Queen's College in the sixth form, and somewhere deep within him he wanted to impress his father. Every term Dalip always came first, second or third in the form, but his father was never impressed, he never seemed to care. Doing well at the G.C.E. Ordinary Level Examination would be a feat that was sure to impress his father. There were also his neighbours: he wanted to *show* them.

When his mother died everything had deteriorated.

Money was difficult because there was at first only one person working and his father spent much of his money on rum and his friends. There was nobody to supervise the boys. They did as they pleased; they played in the avenue with Roy and his friends – who used indecent language frequently and stayed out late at nights laughing and joking. Both Romesh and Dalip fell in with this life very easily.

At first the neighbours complained. Their father would scold them, but after a week or so they continued without thinking anymore of it. The neighbours began to discourage their children from playing with Romesh and Dalip – they were a bad lot – and treat them as though they were outcasts. This had irked Dalip and he told himself that he would show the neighbours that he could do better than all their sons and daughters.

In school he did not bother much with girls; only at term ends, after tests, would he relax and flirt.  Once school re-opened for a new term he forgot about his escapades of the previous term. Sometimes he played cricket, but he was never exceptionally good at any aspect of the game. He was not even a passable batsman, but he kept wicket just competently. On occasions girls would send him notes he never bothered with. He was secretly shy of girls, he felt he did not know how to handle them. However, in the third term in the third form, just after examinations were finished, when one of the girls in his form told him that her friend in the second form liked him, he was eager to know who the girl was. He learnt that she was called Chandra, but the name meant nothing to him. When, however, Chandra was pointed out to him he was pleased. He had noticed her the previous term and liked her immediately. She was tall and slim and quiet; she did not mix with the other girls much. He had looked at her now and again and lately, in the light of what he had been told, he thought she had looked tenderly at him. He told the girl in his form that he liked Chandra too. She decided to arrange a meeting.

The next day the girl told him to follow her. They went to the technical drawing room. She ushered him in and told

79

him to have a good time and left him saying she would be back in five minutes. At first he thought the room was empty, then he saw a movement in the far corner. When he looked carefully he saw Chandra sitting on a stool watching him. He panicked. He did not know what to do or say. How should he begin? What should he tell her? He had not moved from the door. This was too sudden. He did not expect this. If anybody came in the room and saw him speaking to her what would they think? He knew he must do something. He started to walk across the room towards her. He walked slowly, deliberately, so as to give himself time to map out in his head some course of action. He was still undecided when he reached her. It was the first time he had been in a room with a girl he liked, with nobody else around. He pulled a stool close to her and sat facing her, though not too close. He asked her how she was doing. She said fine. She smiled. He could not get out another word or even move his finger in his excitement and the unexpectedness of the encounter. Then there was a knock. Dalip was glad it was the girl from his form. Before he could get up Chandra walked out of the room. She did not look back. The girl from his form shook her head and asked him if he did not do anything. She laughed and they left the room together. Chandra rarely ever looked at him again, and when she looked, her stares were cold.

When Dalip had gone into the fourth form there were new faces – boys and girls. There was one girl he was attracted to. She did not live far from the school. She was short and plump, not fat, but plump, an attractive plumpness. She was always neatly dressed and that attracted Dalip, but she was always so severe. She never seemed to smile and meddle much with the other girls in the form. Dalip was glad of this. Most of the girls in the form had their boyfriends in the fifth form or in the sixth form and in two instances out of the school – not school boys – working men. By the end of the second term he noticed her smiling on occasion with the other girls and saying hi to each other. Then the boys in the form started to hint that Bano (short for Banmattie) and he suited each other. They were both small. The third term was, of course, examination term. Dalip bothered with no one, least of all Bano. At the end of the term, just after the test and just after his Cha Cha died, the girls joined the boys in a card game. They decided not to have two boys on one side since the boys were thought to be the better players and would win most of the games. When they paired themselves, Dalip found the girls had thrust Bano on him, the boys merrily agreeing. Bano blushed and he blushed too. They played about two games until the bell went for the dismissal of school. For the remainder of the week, the girls in the form kept telling Dalip that Bano liked him. Nothing further happened. School closed for August.

When school reopened, Dalip promised himself that until he had written his examinations the next June, he would not go once to the cinema. He told Roy this, who seemed to approve. He promised himself that he would be the best student that year. He attacked his school work keenly; he did assignments promptly and was one of the few students to hand them all in on time, and he got the best grades and marks. He liked mathematics. Sometimes, as his teacher advised, he would work out *all* the problems in a particular exercise while most of the students did only the minimum. He hardly noticed Bano.

Before school closed for Christmas they had to pay their G.C.E. fees. Dalip insisted that he wanted to enter all eight subjects being offered. The headmaster cautioned, but Dalip insisted and after looking at his performance the headmaster agreed. Only three students were allowed to write eight subjects that year.

Before school closed for the Christmas holidays, after the end of term examinations, there was the normally free week when teachers were busy marking papers and preparing reports and when the students played games and had a lively time. Through the internal mail system of the school Dalip got two Christmas cards. One was unsigned; the other, from Bano, had a short note about her love for him. He felt elated when he opened this second one. It was the first time in his life when someone he liked sent him a note of love. But he was sad. Sad because he had to let this go without following it up.

Some of the girls asked why he was avoiding Bano, as he had been after receiving the note. He did not know how to answer. How could he tell them and her that he loved her but that he could not think of her at this point in his life, that his books must come first. How could he tell Bano that her parents had some money and could afford to give her a start in life while his father had nothing to give him, that he must make his own mark and that it was mainly due to his brother he had come so far? How could he tell her that he loved her but could think of her only after the examinations, only after he had achieved good grades? How could he tell her his examination meant the world to him, that it would decide his future, that if he did not do well, he would probably become a drunkard like his father, probably a bum in life? He thought that if he did not get good grades he could never have faith in himself or God anymore, that he would not be worthy of her love. He said none of that, he just avoided her. But when he promised himself that he would keep his distance but be on good terms with her, he found this impossible.

He kept his distance all right, but did not remain on good terms. When he meant to smile, he found himself looking crossly at her, knowing she probably thought he hated her. But he did not hate her, he felt her hurting, he felt her pain. Sometimes he could feel her wanting to cry. Yet he could not go and speak to her and he started to blame her and the girls for wanting to distract him from his schoolwork.

The next term he was absorbed in his work, and she seemed to be studying hard too. He did not have time to think of her much and she, it appeared, did not have time for him. He knew she still felt something for him, but she went out of her way to make it known to Dalip and the form that she did not care.

When the examinations started, Dalip discussed each paper he did with Roy. He estimated the amount of marks he felt he had obtained for each question and totalled the marks.

He reckoned that he would pass all the subjects he wrote, with three distinctions. He told Roy this matter-of-factly. Roy seemed to believe him.

After their G.C.E. examinations ended, the boys planned to go back to school for the remaining week before school closed for August. Some of the girls had decided to go back too. They played games and discussed what they would do after school; they helped teachers with their reports and registers and tried to be useful. Bano was not in school and Dalip did not waste time waiting around for her to come or wishing that she would come. Time was too short and he felt happy and carefree after the examinations. Yet he had thought of going to see her; she did not live far from school, but he was afraid of what her parents would say, and how she would receive him. At nights he would think about visiting her, but in the morning and during the day in school he was always involved with something else. Indeed, he soon found someone else who held his attention. She was in the second form. She was well developed with rounded hips and very noticeable breasts, and when she looked at him he felt desire race in him. Even more to his delight he found he had no difficulty speaking with her – and she responded. They talked in empty formrooms. He held her fingers when nobody was looking. One afternoon a teacher noticed them behind a screen. He was about to investigate when Dalip heard the voice of another teacher, a senior master, telling the teacher to leave the students alone. It was the voice of his literature teacher and Dalip suspected that he had noticed when they had gone into the room. They could do nothing in the room except steal a quick kiss or two, because anyone walking in the corridor could see them from their thighs downwards behind the screen. Dalip knew that this teacher liked him; he felt safe for the remainder of the week. The girl and Dalip had photographs taken behind the school by one of the boys who had walked with his camera. The boys had insisted that Dalip put his arm around Savita. He was too glad to comply. He put his arm around her shoulders for one picture and around her waist for the other. He had squeezed

83

her waist.

On the last day of school she told him she would have to go into school on the following Monday, along with other students of her class, to collect their reports which had not yet been completed. He told her he would be in school around ten.

He was there at ten. Savita had collected her report and was lingering with three other girls. Two teachers were working on their registers in a form room. The rest of the school was empty. He took her into an empty class room. Her friends went into another form room. Dalip did not know quite how they got there, but he found himself lying on a bench with his head resting on her lap. He had one arm round her waist and they were making plans about the next term. She told him how to meet her in their shop and gave him directions. Then Dalip sat up beside her. He sat touching her. Before she could move his hand away it was under her skirt. She tried to move it but could not. He felt the opening and the bump there; it felt very hard. He put a finger between the opening. She started to moan and begged him to remove his hand. When she started to cry he did so. He heard giggles from the next room. He suspected Savita's friends were peeping but he did not care. When Savita had stopped crying he fingered her face. There was a cut on her right cheek and he started playing with it. Then without thinking he grabbed her and embraced her. She did not resist. He pressed his lips on hers, he felt her respond and return the pressure and kiss. Then she jerked away; her friends were knocking on the door. It was the first time that he had kissed a girl.

During the holidays Dalip went to the shop. He became acquainted with Savita's sister who helped in the shop. She was very pretty and like himself had just written her G.C.E. examinations and was awaiting the results. Dalip often went and spoke to the sister. When Savita's mother came into the shop he would pretend he had come to purchase something. Savita never came down into the shop. She had told him that she rarely did, that instead she did most of the housework. Their house was huge. Downstairs there were actually three businesses: a grocery store, a general store and a bar. Savita's father operated the bar; none of the sisters ever went in there. Savita had two sisters apart from the one Dalip was familiar with. She knew Dalip liked Savita. Before he left she would run upstairs and tell Savita. Every time he rode out of the yard, she would hurry to the window, smiling and waving to him, and then hurry back into the house. That was enough for Dalip. This continued until school reopened.

When school reopened Dalip was a hero. Results were out. Dalip and one other boy had passed all eight subjects, both of them had three distinctions. He saw Savita in school that first day but he did not get a chance to speak to her. He waved to her as he hurried out of school to share the news with his father and Roy. His history teacher had told him that he could be admitted to Queen's College to write the London G.C.E. Advanced level examination and had told him how to go about that task. He told Dalip to return to him if he needed help. That midday Dalip told Roy about his results. Roy hugged him and congratulated him. Dalip was happy because Roy was very happy and proud of him. It never crossed his mind that Roy could be or would be anything else. Dalip felt he owed it all to Roy anyway. They began discussing what Dalip should do now. Roy asked Dalip what he thought was best. Dalip told him what his history teacher had advised. He told Roy that if he got good grades he could get a scholarship to study either at the University of Guyana, the University of the West Indies or some British or North American University, to study economics or anything related to Law. When Dalip mentioned Law, Roy looked more closely at him. Then Dalip remembered something. Roy bent his head. All this time while they were talking he had eaten nothing. Dalip felt tears come to his eyes. He remembered his mother; she would have been proud of him now; she would have been the happiest woman in the world just then. He remembered the long conversations she used to have with them under the house, while they waited for Dalip's father to come home. He remembered how his mother had wished that he would do law. Then Roy looked up. His face was serious and without its usual smile. He asked quietly, 'Do you want to go on to the sixth form at Queen's College? Or do you want to get a job? You could get a good job at the one of the banks.'

'What about Daddy? I think he might want me to work. You know how he grumble about money,' Dalip replied weakly. He knew his father would want him to get a job.

'Forget Daddy. What do *you* want? D'you want to be a qualified somebody or stay as you are? Remember, I'll support whatever you want to do.'

'I want to go to Queen's College. I've always wanted to. I intend to do well. I want to win a scholarship to go on to some University,' Dalip blurted out.

'Good. Then that's settled,' Roy said. 'I'm proud of you, Dalip. I'd have liked to do what you're doing. Mommy would've been proud of you. I know you're going to do well at Queen's College.'

'I haven't been admitted yet...'

'You will, you'll see. I think you will fulfil Mommy's wish.'


Then their father's motorcycle was heard. Both were silent. Dalip was wondering how his father would take the news. He felt that his father should be proud of him, at least he was hoping for this. His father entered the house. Both boys greeted him. Before he could go in his room to take off his shirt, as was his habit, Roy addressed him.

'Daddy, Dalip has got his results. He passed all eight subjects with three distinctions. He is the best student for his school this year.'

'Good,' their father said, 'Good.' He smiled. A rare smile, thought Dalip. 'You can get a good job at one of the banks before this month...'

'No, Daddy. Dalip is going back to school.'

'What? Back to school? What for?'

'To Queen's College, to write the 'A' levels.'

'He could get a good job with what he's got now. He

could get more money than I get now...'

'Daddy, don't you think we should allow Dalip to go as far as he can go...'

Roy was interrupted by his father.

'I never went anywhere. I had to come out of school to work in the canefields of Sophia backdam...'

'So Dalip must do the same thing?'

'It would not be the same thing. He would be getting a good job.' His father was silent. Roy was silent. Since his father had come in Dalip had not spoken a word. He waited. His future lay in Roy's hands now. If only he could convince his father.

'Isn't one person enough for you? I had to leave school because you did not care for me.' Roy's voice was almost a whisper. 'Daddy, must Dalip come out of school too because you don't care for him? Daddy, why have you never liked Dalip and me? You always liked Romesh more than the two of us. Why? What have we done you?' Roy spoke softly. There were tears in his eyes.

'Who say I don't like you and Dalip? You don't know how much I suffer because of you boys. I never bring another woman in this house after your mother died because I feel you wouldn't like that. Think that was easy for me...?

'Do you think mommy would like us having to take Dalip out of school when he is doing so well? We don't need Dalip to work to manage. If mommy was alive and Dalip or Romesh wanted to go to school, even if she had to starve and eat bare rice she would've sent them to school. Is because we don't have a mother?' Roy could not continue, the tears starting to flow down his face. Their father went in the bedroom and closed the door. Roy bent his head down on the breakfast table. Dalip felt helpless and angry. Any other father would have been proud and happy. His father did not care. Dalip wanted to comfort Roy. He wanted to tell Roy not to worry, that he had done enough. But he could not say anything. All he could do was stretch across the table and hold Roy's arm. How long they stayed like that Dalip had no idea. He heard the door open quietly. He did not look up. He did not want to see his father's face. He stared at the surface of the breakfast table. He saw a movement. He looked up to see his father's hand on Roy's shoulder almost simultaneously he felt his father's hand on his own shoulder. Roy looked up. Dalip looked up. Their father's eyes were red.

'Congratulations, Dalip,' he said tenderly. 'You will go to Queen's College.'

Dalip could not believe his ears and eyes. He felt gratitude and compassion for his father. Without thinking he jumped up. Almost simultaneously Roy jumped up. They both hugged their father. He put his arms round both of them and squeezed them.

'I'm sorry, Daddy,' Roy murmured. He was crying again.

'Thanks, Daddy... Thanks...' Dalip was crying too. He buried his face on his father's shoulder. The last time he hugged his father had been before his mother died. He noted that Roy was now slightly taller than his father. That was how Romesh found them. He was laughing.

'What happening, everybody?' Romesh asked.

'Your brother has passed his exams. He will be going to Q.C.,' said their father, releasing Roy and Dalip.

'Congrats. Dalip, you always were a lucky ba...' he stopped. Laughing he continued, 'Don't forget that you aren't the only person who can pass exams. I just learnt that I've passed the P.C. examinations in English, Maths, Literature, History, Geography and Woodwork. Mr. Singh said I could be admitted to a secondary school in the third form if you go into the Ministry and look after the matter.' Dalip, Roy and their father exchanged looks.

'Congrats yourself,' Dalip said. He felt happy. Romesh was walking towards them.

'What about my hug, Daddy?' Their father hugged him. Instinctively both Roy and Dalip touched their father. Romesh laughed.

'Dalip, up to now we still not the same, eh!' Dalip knew

what he meant. They had always competed for their father's affection.

'I will go into the Ministry and find out about Romesh...' Roy began.

'No. I shall do that and Dalip's as well,' their father said firmly.

In a flash Dalip remembered something he thought he had forgotten. He remembered when they had first moved into Margaret Street, their father had taken both he and Romesh to be admitted to the nearby primary school. He had thought that unusual. He had found even more unusual the kindness of their father that day. In a way it would be just like that again – except that he would be going to Queen's College and Romesh to another secondary school.

# Chapter Six

Within the week Romesh was admitted to a secondary school and Dalip to Queen's College. Dalip was happy, he had achieved his dream. He was a student there now – no, not a mere student, but a sixth former. Not many persons were admitted to the sixth form at Queen's College. This success, however, was not the only cause of Dalip's happiness. His father had taken them to a tailor who took measurements to make two school shirts and school pants for each of the boys. It was the first time his father had taken such an interest in him, and he loved his father for this.

Dalip had opted to do Economics, History and English Literature. He did not know exactly what he would do later, but it would be something to do with Economics (Banking or Management) or Law. The book list was long and the books expensive, but his father did not hesitate to purchase the books, and for the first time since Dalip had known him, he had not grumbled about 'things being hard'. That alone was worth all the work he had done, all the sacrifices he had made.

Dalip got on well at school; he learnt quickly and before the end of the first term he was familiar with most of Queen's College and felt that he belonged there. Before the end of the first term, Roy bought a motorcycle and he gave Dalip his shiny, almost new bicycle. Dalip gave his own cycle, which had been his mother's, to Romesh. Roy also had Dalip take out a provisional licence and taught him how to ride. Before long his father allowed Dalip to ride his motorcycle too whenever he was not using it. His father had never cared much about cleaning his motorcycle, but every Sunday, after Roy finished cleaning his, Dalip, with help from Romesh would wash and polish their father's. Dalip did not ride his father's motorcycle often, he liked riding something looking clean and flashy.

Once a week Roy would take Romesh and Dalip to the cinema. These were mainly night shows because Roy came home late from work in the afternoons. They always enjoyed these occasions, walking to the cinema, Roy showing them bars, restaurants, hotels, and explaining how they operated. Dalip remembered then how he and Roy had walked to and from the library on Saturdays when their mother was alive. Often Roy's friends would go with them to the cinema. Like Roy, they were all working; they were noisy and jovial, teasing girls on the road or waving to girls they did not know. Sometimes the girls waved back. Dalip liked being with them. Like Roy, the boys enjoyed an occasional beer but they did not touch rum and were mostly moderate. They always went into the stalls, or pit as they called it, when they went to the cinema. This was how Dalip saw most of his films.

He did not have much money. Roy could just afford to give both Romesh and himself two dollars a week as pocket money. Dalip saved most of it. Roy seemed freer with money, as did his father. Now that they did not have to pay school fees for him, there was a little more money to spare.

Dalip thought that another reason why his father seemed to have more money was because he had eased his drinking considerably. At first the boys had not noticed this until they found their father helping with the cooking in the afternoons with increasing frequency. They were happy that their father came home more often. He still, once, sometimes twice a week, came home late and slightly drunk, but the boys did not mind that much. When he did not come home early, Dalip always found himself waiting for his father. He would have one of his school books open in front of him, but he was always listening for the throb of his father's motorcycle. He felt that it was the same with Roy and Romesh. They would have books in front of them but he felt that, like him, they were waiting for their father. Nobody ever admitted this waiting. Dalip thought he knew why, that it reminded them of their mother when she too used to wait on their father. When Dalip heard his father's motorcycle he would feel relieved. From then on he found he could concentrate more on his work. Roy would get up immediately, put on the downstairs light and go downstairs to help his father up if he needed assistance and put the motorcycle safely in the storeroom under the house.

When their father came home early he would sometimes sit by himself and take a drink or two from the bottle of rum he kept in the cupboard. Though the boys did not like him drinking rum, they felt much better that he did this at home, where he was safe, and where, of course, he spent much less money.

Romesh had also adapted quickly to his school and was doing well, according to what he said and what his report showed. Roy had been speaking of learning bookkeeping. He bought some books and two afternoons a week he went to bookkeeping classes. Dalip felt happy at nights when he looked up to find Roy working at his bookkeeping or reading a magazine, and Romesh reading some book or doing his homework. Even their father would sometimes sit with them; he would read magazines – he read comics also -- especially war comics. Romesh, Roy and Dalip read these comics too for relaxation. They often discussed the books they read and liked it when their father joined in these discussions. He would tell them how, when he was a boy during the second world war, there had once been great excitement when a German submarine came into the Demerara River. He would also tell them how food commodities had been rationed. Once he started discussing the war it did not take long for him to start speaking of other things, of how as a boy he had worked in the canefields of Sophia.

He would tell them about his father, their Aja, who was still alive, and his stepmother. He would tell them how she used to treat him and his brother. Dalip had never known that their Ajee was their father's stepmother; he had always thought that she was his father's real mother.

They asked him when his mother died. He told them he did not know exactly, but he thought he had been about five years old. This was all strange and exciting for the boys and they would flood him with questions.

One night he brought out the mandoline he had in his room. As long as Dalip remembered he had seen the instrument in his father's room but he had never heard his father play it. His father started to tune it. He hummed a few lines of an old Hindi song. He started to play in time. He played a quarter of a song and then stopped. He started a number of songs but always stopped shortly after starting them. He still played magnificently, and even from the brief snatches of the songs, Dalip knew he had never heard anything so beautiful before and that his father had a most melodious voice. His father then stopped, shaking his head. He flexed his fingers and said it was because he had not played for such a long time. He murmured something about rum and his reflexes. Then he told them about the mandoline. He had played it before he married their mother and had sung too, even on the radio on occasions. Dalip felt he was beginning to see a side of his father he could not only like, but respect and admire. He began to see why his mother had fallen in love with him and had loved him so strongly. Was it not happening to him too? After that night their father left the mandoline outside saying they could practice with it; he would be very pleased if one of them would learn to play the instrument. That was more than enough for Dalip. He monopolised the mandoline for most of the time. His father showed him how to play and told him he must learn the notes and scales first before trying to play any tune. In his spare time Dalip practised and practised.

When their father was not present, Roy, Dalip and Romesh would discuss him. The others seemed to feel as Dalip was feeling about him. It was at such times that they realised that he had cared about them all along, even though he had not shown it openly. It was then that they started to realise how much it must have cost him, and was perhaps still costing him, not to have brought another woman home, not taking another wife. From what he said about his stepmother, they knew he was determined that they should not suffer at a stepmother's hands, as he had suffered, and he had done this at his own expense. Even then he was not an old man. Dalip guessed his father to be about forty-two or forty-three and that when their mother died he must have been about thirty-two or thirty-three. It must have been even harder then. Then Roy reminded them that when their mother was alive he had always gotten up early in the mornings to help her cook and many times cooked on his own. Since their mother died he had been doing it every day of every week with the exception of Sundays – when he cooked late because everyone was at home and because they all got up later. Roy asked them who they thought he did this for. There was no need to answer.

Recently, too, Dalip found that he was becoming even more attached to Roy. What Roy said about his father was perhaps even more applicable to himself. Roy did, and had done, many things for Dalip and Romesh, as he did for everyone else, without consideration of himself. Dalip sometimes felt that it was Roy's one desire to see that he and Romesh got a good education. Roy always put himself last. He helped the neighbours when they needed help, always with a smile. Everyone liked him, but he had one peculiarity.

He seemed to take pleasure in scaring all the little children in the neighbourhood. He would screw up his eyes and make a frightening face. The little boys and girls would run away from him when he did this. It was always fun to watch him do it. Dalip always sensed the laughter behind the frightening face. As soon as the child ran off, scared and sometimes crying, Roy would burst into laughter. No parent ever reprimanded him for this.

One night, as Roy was going to the toilet, he fell. There was a loud crash. Dalip rushed to see what had happened, followed by Romesh. Their father was already there beside Roy, who was senseless on the floor. His father had got limacol and was rubbing Roy with it. Roy revived. He looked around dazed. He put his head in his hands for a while. His father asked him what had happened. Roy told them he had just 'blacked-out' and had fallen. He said he felt dizzy and agreed with their father's suggestion that he should see a doctor the next day.

The doctor told him he was weak and bilious and needed rest. He was given some tablets and two weeks sick leave. Roy gave them the impression that nothing was wrong, that he would soon be well again, that it was just a minor illness which rest would cure. Most afternoons when he came home from school Dalip would find Roy reading in the hammock downstairs or dozing. Sometimes Dalip found him staring out at the blue sky and he seemed to be deep in contemplation. There was something sad about him then. When he realised that Dalip was observing him, he seemed surprised, but would quickly become his old jovial self again. Then he had taken to wearing dark glasses. At first Dalip took no notice of that, thinking that he wore them against the glare of the sun when he looked at the sky, but he began to feel that there was something else, that Roy was hiding something.

Then one afternoon when he came home from school – he remembered it was the first day of June – he could not see Roy anywhere around. He was puzzled and checked the rooms one by one, but Roy was nowhere. He was looking about the neighbourhood, to see if Roy had gone visiting, when Romesh came home. Romesh searched too. Puzzled, they returned home with a deepening unease. Shortly after four o'clock their father came home. He told them that Roy had been admitted to hospital. Dalip felt sick. He wanted to cry. In a second, the thought raced into his mind: Roy will die. And Roy knows he will die. Whenever in the past they had visited anyone in hospital, Roy had always said to Romesh and Dalip afterwards that he did not ever want to go into hospital as a patient; he feared that, if he were ever admitted to hospital, he would die. Dalip understood what Roy said because he felt exactly the same. His father explained that their aunt Sattie had heard that Roy was ill and had come to see him during the day. She had been puzzled at him wearing dark glasses and had insisted that

95

he take them off. She said it made him appear frightening. When he took off the glasses she saw that his eyes were yellow instead of white. It looked bad. She suspected immediately that he had jaundice. She knew of people who had been killed by it so she insisted that he go with her to the hospital immediately. The doctor had given Roy one look and admitted him right away. He told Aunt Sattie that three more days and Roy would have been dead; it was serious. She had then informed Dalip's father.

They closed the house and left for the hospital, taking some clothes and pajamas for Roy. When they found him, Roy was in good spirits, laughing and chattering with some of their cousins who were seated around the bed.

When Dalip asked how he was keeping he said fine, just fine, and laughed. He told him to bring his transistor the next day and the novel he was reading. It must have been very hard for Roy, Dalip thought, yet he was smiling, he who had never wanted to be admitted to a hospital, who had felt that if he was ever admitted it would be to die.

The doctors told them that they could bring food if they wanted, but they must not bring fatty foods or foods which might upset Roy or cause him to vomit, but that they could bring him anything to drink.

The next day Dalip went early and took the radio and the book. They talked. Dalip examined Roy's eyes which were yellowish. Even the palms of his hands and the soles of his feet had a yellow hue. Roy spoke of the pretty nurses, with a mischievous twinkle in his eyes. But it seemed to Dalip that Roy did not want him to ask any questions while they were alone, and that he felt relief when the bedside filled up rapidly. Dalip had not realised they had so many relatives. On the third day there was a lightness in Roy's eyes; the yellow had faded considerably and the dyed hue of his palms and the soles of his feet was only just visible. Everyone commented on this. Roy was, as usual, in good spirits; he laughed and joked and chatted and made everybody feel lively. Even Dalip felt better, but deep within him there was a fear and a doubt, and not just a small nagging doubt. But he kept his fear to himself. He knew that if he told anybody that he felt that Roy would not get well and if Roy actually died, people would think he was the cause of the death and that he had a 'black tongue'. These were horrid days for Dalip; he could hardly concentrate on his school work or any work for that matter. During that time he prayed that he was wrong and that everybody else was right.

The doctor told his father that Roy was out of danger. The next day it seemed that Roy had improved slightly. Everybody said so. Dalip did not agree with them, he was convinced that Roy remained the same as the previous day, but he did not dare contradict everybody else's optimism. He did not even discuss his fears with Romesh and he hardly had a chance to speak to Roy that afternoon. There was the usual large crowd of relatives and a girl called Josephine. Roy had spoken a lot about her to Romesh and Dalip. Dalip knew that Roy would want to be with her, so he left the bed and wandered about the hospital, talking to the nurses on duty, some of whom he had got to know quite well. He asked the nurse on duty if he could come back about eight o'clock that night to check his brother. She told him that visitors were not permitted then. When he replied that he was aware of that or he would not have asked, she smiled and said that if he got past the guard he could come. He asked for her name – Jannet Singh. He made a mental note of it and told her his.

Around eight o'clock that night, he and Romesh set off for the hospital on their father's motorcycle. When they arrived Romesh said that he did not want to go in, that he would remain downstairs. Dalip told him he would be upstairs for only about five minutes. Dalip went up to the guard saying that he wanted to give Miss Jannet Singh a message. The guard looked uncertain, but let him upstairs. He walked quickly to the duty room where he found Jannet and other nurses. She smiled, asking how he had managed to get in. He told her he would just see his brother for a moment and then he would tell her. When he reached Roy's bed he saw that he was asleep. He seemed restless, but nothing too unusual and after about a minute, which seemed like an hour, he went back to the duty room. He chatted with the nurses and told Jannet that he had been allowed in because he had told the guard that he had wanted to see her and – he added without thinking – that was really why he had come, she was very pretty. It was true in a way, she was pretty, but he could not tell her that he had really come because something about Roy was bothering him, something he could not identify. He left. He thanked the guard and told Romesh that Roy was sleeping. When they got home his father enquired and Dalip told him the same thing.

The next afternoon Dalip was late. When he went in Jannet did not smile. She looked sadly at him before returning his greeting. He hurried to Roy's bedside. He almost froze. Everybody, it seemed, was standing outside the three-quarter wall which bordered Roy's bed. Dalip knew that something was wrong. His first thought was that Roy was dead. He hurried up. There was a screen around the bed and somebody said that he could not go in, that his aunts were changing Roy. Then Romesh materialised from a corner. He put his arm around Dalip and told him that Roy was unconscious and had been so for most of the day. He had been conscious at about ten when he ate, then he had gone to sleep. He had woken at midday when their father visited. Roy had told his father to tell Dalip thanks for going to see him the night before. When Romesh told him this, Dalip could not believe it. He was positive that Roy had been asleep when he visited him, there could be no doubt in his mind about that. True, Roy had seemed restless, but he was asleep all the same. If he had been awake he would have spoken to him. How could Roy have known that he had been there? Jannet most likely must have told him. Then his thoughts froze. Jannet came off duty at eleven; the nurses who worked the shifts when Roy was conscious could not have known that he had entered the ward that night. Perhaps one of the patients had seen him and told Roy, but Romesh had said that almost immediately Roy had eaten he had gone back to sleep; still, somebody must have told Roy about his visit, but no patient could have seen him when he was in the corridor and nobody else had been in the corridor. He remembered distinctly that his shoes had made no sound on its concrete floor in the silent night. He would have noted any other thing, any other sound. He prided himself on his ability to observe, to see when others did not see. It had started in literature classes; his teacher was constantly pointing out that most of the good writers, apart from the quality of their writing, had the ability to notice everything. They *saw* when they looked. The teacher encouraged those of the boys who thought of becoming writers, especially poets, to look at things and see 'consciously'. He had been practising that. Whenever he did something or went anywhere, especially if it was not part of his normal experience, he trained himself to note everything. The night before was the first time in his life that he had been in a hospital at night.

Could it have been that when he was waiting, Roy's soul was out of his body hovering in the room and had seen everything that had happened? That was not impossible. Dalip had always heard the old people say that the soul wandered and that while a person was sleeping his soul left his body. That was why they said that when someone was sleeping another person should not attempt to shake them awake suddenly, but make some noise or call two or three times before touching or shaking the person. Dalip had always thought that this was one of the many superstitious beliefs that the old Hindus had. But the more he had been reading of late, the less emphatic he was in saying that these things were nonsense. Had he not read recently of documented instances in the United States where patients who were being operated on, and were unconscious, had told the doctors exactly what had happened during the operation? This had happened, while not frequently, often enough for a doctor to document as many of the instances as were known and write a whole book on the subject, citing facts, dates, names, places and conversations...

Dalip said nothing to Romesh, but instead asked why Roy was being changed, and Romesh explained that Roy had wet himself in his sleep about four times since about one

99

o'clock and the nurses would soon attach a catheter into his penis to ease the problem of having him wet his clothing and the bed. What was the use loitering outside the room? Roy was unconscious. Yet everybody loitered, everybody stayed outside in the corridor, even Dalip, though he was finding it unbearable. He felt like screaming, like stamping. He had to move about, he could not stay in one place. He tried to appear calm, he tried to talk as the others were doing, but he could not. He told Romesh he was going for a walk. He walked up and down in the hospital and this calmed him a little. He tried to look and register what he saw and this helped. He saw people with broken arms and legs, some slung in awkward positions. This made him want to laugh. In some rooms he saw people on saline drips. Others sat around helpless, watching, waiting with sad faces. Why should people be sad at death, he thought, death was inevitable, at any rate, one should not mourn at death.

At Queen's College he had become an active member of the Hindu society. This group had organised many discussions on the Hindu scriptures – especially the *Bhagavad Gita*. He remembered the discourse between Lord Krishna and Arjuna on death. Krishna told Arjuna that he should not fear death. Dalip recalled the verse in Chapter Two of the *Gita*, '... the death of him who is born is certain; and the rebirth of him who is dead is inevitable. It does not, therefore, behove you to grieve over an inevitable event.' And another verse went, 'The soul is never born nor dies...' Once they had long and heated discussions on verse fifteen of Chapter Two, the verse where Krishna tells Arjuna, 'Arjuna, the wise men to whom pleasure and pain are alike, and who are not tormented by these contrasts, become eligible for immortality.' During the discussion on this verse Dalip had argued that this was an impossible task and that anybody who could achieve it was a man not only to be respected, but worshipped, because such a person would be God. But they had all resolved to try to attain this state or come as close to it as possible. Now, however, he was not doing anything of the sort. He was becoming emotional. No. He must try to control himself and his emotions. This would be difficult, but at least he should try. He tried as determinedly as he could that afternoon and was so engrossed in his thoughts that when he passed the duty room he did not see Jannet looking intently at him as he passed.

The next day was a Friday. When Dalip went into the hospital, Roy was no longer there. The bed was empty. The room was empty. There were no relatives or friends around. Dalip, attempting to calm himself, tried to walk unhurriedly to the nurses' duty room. The first person he saw was Jannet. He spoke softly, 'What has happened to Roy?'

'He is in another room. Go north.' She pointed. 'The second room on the left.'

'Thanks. How are you? I didn't see you yesterday...'

'I am all right, but I know you are not. Yesterday you looked straight at me and didn't see me.' She added almost laughing, 'You almost looked crazy yesterday afternoon, wandering about the wards.'

'I'm sorry. I did not mean...'

'That's understandable. If I can help, let me know. I will be willing to.'

'Thanks. I will come back before I go.'

'I hope so.'

Dalip smiled and set off for the room that Roy was in. Roy looked calm, as though he was having a sleep he was enjoying. He was being given a saline drip. Everybody was silent. The doctor had said there was a good chance that Roy would recover and everyone looked as though they wanted to believe this. Dalip wanted to laugh. He knew that Roy would never recover. He knew he was staring at a dead man. Strange, he did not feel sad or worried; he felt calm and relaxed as he looked at Roy's face. The face seemed to have a smile, he thought. Dalip left the room, but the moment he left it he felt sad. When he reached the duty room Jannet was alone.

'Hi. Come in. Sit down.' She smiled.

Dalip liked her. 'You are thoughtful. Your boyfriend is a lucky man.'

'Thanks,' she blushed. 'He *was* lucky, but he didn't think so.'

'You mean you don't have a boyfriend?' Dalip felt excited. She had said *was*, but he wanted to be sure.

'No,' she said pleasantly.

'I wish...'

'Nothing is stopping you,' she interrupted.

'Yes, I don't work...'

'I know.'

'How?'

'Your brother, Roy.'

'What did he....'

'Many things that are not important now,' and as an afterthought and teasing, 'Don't worry – nothing bad.'

Dalip smiled.

'Tomorrow is my day off. I know that you might not have money but be practical and don't think about pride – let's go out tomorrow. It's Saturday tomorrow, you won't have school and there is nothing much you can do except hope. The expenses are on me.'

'Thanks Jannet. I... I....' Dalip could not find words to tell her that he was grateful, that he did not expect this. She was so beautiful he thought, older than himself, perhaps not very much. He reached over and touched her hand. 'Where tomorrow?'

'We will decide then. How about eleven o'clock?' she asked. He nodded and she continued, 'Under the market clock. Stabroek Market. Okay?'

'Yes, yes....'

'Tomorrow then?'

'Yes, see you tomorrow.' He got up. At the door on impulse he turned and said, 'Have pleasant dreams tonight....' He wanted to add, about me, but he only said, 'I will, about you.'


That night he did not sleep immediately he got in bed. He tossed and turned. However, the tossing and turning was

102

not only on account of Roy.

He was nervous and excited about Jannet. He had never been on a date before – at least not like this – where the girl was evidently more experienced than he was, would be paying the expenses of the outing, was older than he was, was working and was beautiful. He went to sleep thinking of what might happen the next day.

When he reached under the market clock it was five minutes to eleven. He looked all around. She was not there. He tried to recognise her in the crowd constantly milling around him. He thought he saw her many times, but the person always turned out to be somebody else. Then he felt a hand on his arm. He knew it must be her. He was thrilled at the touch. He turned.

'Hi! Waiting long?' she smiled. He could barely recognise her. She was in tight trousers and a loose thin blouse which reached down to her hips. He could almost see through the blouse. Her hair, always rolled up when he saw her on duty in the hospital, was open and hung halfway down her back. It was thick and black, very black. It looked as though it had just been washed. She was more beautiful than he had imagined. The thought passed through his mind, Can this be possible, can I be the person who would be going out with this princess? She was so much like the princesses he had read about in the coloured picture books of his childhood. All she needs now, he thought, is a crown and flowers in her hair – and perhaps a frock. He felt her squeeze his arm.

'I... I.... You are... you are... you...' he stammered and groped for words. This was not how it was in his dreams or in his literature classes, or with the boys discussing or arguing about anything. She smiled and her hand dropped from his arm. Her fingers found his.

His first impulse was to jerk them away. He blushed and felt ashamed. Here, in the open, he wanted to ask – in the heart of the city with a Saturday morning market crowd passing round and about? His eyes left her face for a moment and rested briefly on the crowd. Then he looked at her again, at her dark eyes, her full shapely body. He squeezed her fingers and thought to himself, what if everybody sees. I'm glad if they see. Not everybody can have such a beautiful girl. I am proud that I have a date with her. He felt himself relaxing.

'Where to?' he asked, and though he was serious he said jokingly, 'I've never had a date with anybody before. If I appear awkward please don't mind...'

'Let's go and get something to eat. We have the whole day ahead of us.'

There was something in her voice that bothered him. Whenever she said anything playfully or teasingly he felt some sort of mockery in her voice. But it didn't feel as if it was directed at him, perhaps to herself, perhaps it was just the way she spoke. She was taking him to a restaurant he would like, she said. They walked through the shopping area. There were people everywhere. They held fingers most of the time. Sometimes Dalip found himself placing his arm around her waist to guide her through the crowd when the pavement was too congested. The first time he did this without realising he had done it. After that he put his arm around her waist whenever there was a crowd, and left it there even after they had passed through it. Sometimes, fleetingly, she rested her head on his shoulder – she was almost as tall as he was – then he felt as though someone had passed a warm towel over his body. He was feeling more and more relaxed and comfortable, as though he had been doing this all his life, thanks perhaps to all the love scenes he had read about in books. He wondered if he was making a good imitation. But this was no book, this was real. He was not imitating anybody. He was being guided by some unseen and unknown force. It was like his wicket-keeping. He knew when he first started keeping wicket that he made a conscious effort to pick up the line of the ball as it left the bowler's hand, but after a while he picked up the line without realising he had done it. Before he knew it he would have moved into position and be waiting for the ball. The only difference now was that he had not practised what he was doing at any time in his life – not in this one anyway.

'We must have met....' he started.

'What?' she murmured.

He had spoken his thoughts without meaning to. 'We must have met in another life. I feel as though I have known you.'

'You too...' her voice trailed off.

'Are you Hindu?' Dalip asked.

'Yes. Why?'

'I'm trying to recall a verse from the *Bhagavad Gita*. It's one when Krishna is telling Arjuna that the two of them had met on previous occasions, in previous births....'

'Yes, I remember it – though I can't remember the chapter and verse. Can you?

'No. I'm trying to but I can't right now,' Dalip said.

'Never mind, forget it.' She squeezed him. Afterwards Dalip could never remember exactly how the whole day passed. He remembered being in the restaurant which was at the top of a building and had a view of part of the city. There they had spoken of many things. He was surprised to learn that she was only nineteen, only a year older than he was. He had thought she was much older than that.

'Does it matter much, my being older?' she asked somewhat sadly, he thought.

'No. Not at all. I have always felt that I might end up marrying someone older than myself...'

'Why?'

'You see my mother died before I was ten....'

'I'm sorry,' she said, touching his hand on the table, not caring who saw.

'No need to be sorry – part of life, eh? In the *Bhagavad Gita* Krishna tells Arjuna to look without compassion on life and death in general – and what fuss? She did not care for us...'

'How can you say so?' she asked, taken aback. Dalip was surprised himself. He never realised he felt that way and the bitterness in his voice startled him. These were not his thoughts. He loved his mother, he told himself and he knew

105

his mother had loved them very much but... Before he could control himself he said, 'You see my mother committed suicide. If she had cared for us she wouldn't have done it. No matter how hard her life might have been, if she really loved us she would not have killed herself, she would have put up with life for our sakes...' He said it all very quickly. He had to get it out of him. Even now he experienced a strong and physical feeling of bitterness towards his mother. He made a conscious effort to control himself. Jannet paid the bill and they left. She said she wanted to go to the cinema. Dalip, quite gallantly, he thought, said that if that was what she wanted then that was what they would do. He was regaining his composure, but he was troubled about what he had just realised about himself. But Jannet's hand on his arm, her nearness – sometimes they would walk so close that her leg touched his – all this made him forget his mother.

At the cinema, before she could open her purse, he had purchased the tickets. He had walked with the accumulated savings from his pocket money. He did not feel right about her paying for everything and he felt that he would lose face in front of the crowd if he allowed her to purchase the tickets. He did not *want* to spend the little money he had; he had indeed resolved the night before that he would not spend his money because he felt certain Roy would die. His father would be the sole worker in the house and he would have the burden of funeral expenses – things would be tough financially. Now, however, he did not care – as well as his pride, he felt he would do anything for Jannet. He loved her already. He was starting to feel that he would never love any other person as he loved her. In the cinema, under the cover of darkness, he put his arm around her. He somehow felt safe and reassured in the cinema. She seemed relaxed too. She rested her head on his shoulder as they watched the film. They spoke on occasion, but were happily silent most of the time. Dalip again felt that they had been born for each other. He told her so. He kissed her hair and her cheek fleetingly. He was afraid she might not want him to, that she might object when he rested his hand on her legs. She said or did nothing which expressed displeasure and he cautiously, with his fingers, stroked her legs – or rather her trousers. She moved closer to him when he did this and took his hand in hers and pressed it to her body.

He remembered the time when he had put his hand beneath Savita's dress and deliberately, almost brutally, fingered her. He could not do that to Jannet. For one thing she had trousers on and even if she had had a dress on he did not want to do that to her. He loved her. To do that would be wrong, it would be humiliating her in some way and he could not humiliate her, he would never humiliate her as long as he lived.

He touched his lips to her cheek and she turned. Next he felt her lips on his own. Her tongue touched his own. He opened his lips, her tongue went into his mouth. They moved apart. It was the first time that Dalip had tongued with any-body or, more correctly, was tongued by anybody. He had read about it. It had always made him excited as he read about it but this was different. This was horrid. He wanted to vomit. He could feel her saliva on the edge of his lips still. That made him want to vomit. Casually he took out his handkerchief and wiped his mouth. Later when she turned to him again he did not want to but she did not seem to notice. They kissed. To Dalip's surprise, after about the third time, he started becom-ing more familiar with the kissing and started to enjoy it more. Yet it made him feel tense and before they left the cinema both of them had to relieve themselves.

It was after four when they came out of the cinema. Visiting time at the hospital, Dalip thought. Jannet seemed to have read his mind.

'Time to go...? Are you going straight to the hospital?' she asked.

'No,' he blurted out. He was angry with himself for saying it. He did not want to discuss how he actually felt about his brother – not to anybody. He knew he would have to now. He knew that if there was anybody he could discuss it with it was with Jannet. He felt she could understand. She did not question him, but he felt compelled to tell her how he felt. He could not tell Romesh even, but he could tell her. They bought milk shakes and chicken burgers then walked to the Botanical Gardens. There they sat down under a huge tree on the grass, their backs to the tree trunk which rose like a wall from the ground. On the other side of the tree were two other persons who were sitting close to each other, eating and drinking. Dalip tilted Jannet's straw and drank from it. She smiled and drank from his. In an instant the incident reminded him of his mother, then he remembered what it brought back to him.

'When my mother was alive, every Saturday she used to bake bread. Before she was finished, my younger brother and I used to get pieces of bread and we would race to feed her and once she had taken a bite we would eat the remainder of the bread happily – her "jutha" he quoted the term he had used at home. 'You remind me of my mother,' he said. They had finished eating. Dalip noted that she took the empty milk shake cups and the wrapping of the eaten chicken-burgers and placed them in the paper bag they had brought them in. That was just like his mother. Earlier in the school term when his class were studying *Sons and Lovers*, a book on the 'A' level syllabus, their teacher had pointed out to them that the hero Paul was in love with his mother and that Paul was attracted to Miriam because of her resemblance to his mother. He had told them about the Oedipus complex. Since then Dalip had been conscious of it and on looking back at his life was surprised that unconsciously, all the girls he had been attracted to had some trait or feature of his mother. Since then he had started to get a strange feeling that he would eventually end up marrying someone older than himself and that this woman would be everything to him. In a way he knew he willed it, wanted it to be so. He did not care what society would say.

'That is why I love you, I think.' His head was resting in her lap, her back was to the tree trunk and her legs were slightly parted. He was between those legs, one arm around one leg, the other resting on the ground. He was looking up into her face.

'Why did your mother commit suicide?' she asked gently.

'I don't know. I was always curious. I don't exactly know, but one day I shall find out. There will probably be lots of trouble when I do. I think it will stir up the proverbial hornet's nest. I suspect that my father may be involved and my aunts and my mother's mother, my Nanee. I will do it once I start working and can afford to be on my own. I know it will cause a lot of ill feeling. People will hate me for doing it – the people concerned.' There was silence but Dalip felt happy and contented with life. He heard the songs of different birds. Looking past Jannet's face he saw very white, puffy clouds drift by.

'If only life could remain like this forever!' he hugged Jannet's legs and half turned and kissed her belly through her blouse. She bent and kissed his face, her hair falling over him. He held her neck and pressed her face down. They kissed. That reminded him...

'Jannet, there are so many things I don't know about you. You have had boyfriends before?'

'No. A boyfriend.' She seemed hesitant.

'If you're not bothered about talking about it, or don't think it too personal, do you want to tell...'

'No. I don't think it too personal. If you want to know I will tell. Maybe it's best you know. He was my school teacher in high school. My parents knew. He came home often. They liked him. We went out together often. Then he went away to further his studies. He wrote twice. The last time about a year ago – to say he had gotten married. I had sex with him once. The week before he left. He had promised to marry me.' She was silent, looking at him intently. 'Does it matter? I know you will think...'

'Yes,' he interjected, 'It matters, but not much. Frankly, I thought you might have passed through more than that. I thought you might have had many boyfriends. This is much better than I expected. Did you love him very much?'

'Yes. I suppose so. A schoolgirl's love for her teacher.'

'And if he were to return?'

'I have gotten over him. I know that. I would ignore him or any other man who did what he did to me. I used to think that I could never love another man, but I am falling in love all over again. Deeper and stronger. Stronger than I want to....'

'Why do you say deeper?'

'Because I was then a school girl. Like every other school girl then in my form I just wanted to love and, of course, be loved. I did not know anything of love or men or people. I have learnt I think. Then I did not know what I really wanted. Now I am more certain of myself. I can control myself better. I am loving you with a greater understanding of myself and of you too. As a nurse I have learnt too.'

'Why did you not have a boyfriend after? As a nurse, as a beautiful nurse, many patients and visitors must have been attracted to you.' Dalip felt calm. He felt tender towards her.

She thought for a while then said, 'It is natural that patients should have some attachment to someone who has nursed them. I never took them seriously and I did not want another man. I had not quite gotten over what had happened to me too. The visitors seemed to want me because of my body....'

'How do you know I don't want you because of your body?' Dalip said half-seriously, half-playfully.

'Perhaps you might now, but not when you first saw me. When you first saw me I felt that you were attracted to something in me, not my body. That made the difference. And the other thing was that I wanted to make the choice...'

'Didn't you make the choice the first time?'

'Yes, but unconsciously. I did not make a conscious choice. I did not consider anything about the person.'

'And you have now?'

'Yes.'

'Have you thought about our age? Did you know that I was younger...'

She did not allow him to finish. 'Yes. I knew from Roy. He spoke a lot of you. He likes you very much. He respects

110

you too. He told me how you put your school work in front of everything else. When I first saw you I was attracted but when he spoke of you I suppose that made me start to like you more...'

'What would your parents think?'

'They don't have to know details – at least not until after you write your 'A' levels....' For a while she did not speak. Nor did Dalip. This was beautiful. She was beautiful. He had found his woman. He wanted nobody else in life. She was what he had always wanted. They kissed, they hugged each other. She looked at her watch. He saw that it was a few minutes to six.

'Do you have to go? Couldn't we stay like this forever?'

'No. Not yet anyway. Next week I am off two days, Thursday and Friday.'

'Very well, but they're school days.' He wanted to add that next week was a long way off. He remembered Roy then; he felt weary.

'We could meet in the afternoon.' She smiled and took his hand. They moved out of the Gardens. They took a taxi to the East Coast car park. She lived on the East Coast, about thirty minutes drive from the city. She waved from the car. He waved and blew a kiss. Her cheeks coloured. The car receded.

Instinctively he turned to the West. The clouds were red in the sky. The sun was down. The day was dying. He thought of Roy.

Nobody asked him where he had been or why he had not gone to the hospital, though Romesh looked at him strangely as though he wanted to ask. Dalip tried to read that night but could not. Romesh watched him and said nothing. Dalip thought constantly of Roy. He knew that he would not recover. How he knew he did not know, but he was convinced. The waiting was terrible and the knowledge was terrible. He should have discussed it with Jannet. He had been on the point of discussing it with her but something else had entered his mind. What was it? He could not remember. Ah! But wasn't

111

she beautiful. She was not a virgin. Strange that it did not disturb him. Maybe he was growing up. Once he had thought his wife must be a virgin when he married her, now many things seemed not to matter anymore. The one year he had spent in the sixth form had changed him a lot. He could begin to look back on his childhood with some clarity, even at himself. He knew his awareness of things and people had increased.

Roy, Roy, Roy! Roy, why do you have to die now? He wanted to shout. He knew he would not sleep well that night. He wanted to go for a walk but he did not. He did not feel like thinking more than he had already thought, of Roy and now Jannet. He always thought more – and more clearly too – in the night, especially if the place was silent or he walked in the avenue.

The next day, Sunday, Dalip woke late as usual. He was restless. After noon he could not even wash and polish his father's motorcycle. That would be too painful, it would remind him of Roy. He went for a ride and realised that the cycle he was riding was once Roy's. The shirt he was wearing was bought by Roy. Could he not get away from Roy? He was exasperated. He knew that if he was someone who consumed alcohol he would have gone and gotten drunk. Maybe that was why his father used to drink so much after his mother's death. But that would not solve the problem. It would blank his mind for a few hours, but afterwards... He was tempted to go and get drunk all the same. He needed a few hours relief from his dread. He wished that Jannet was free. Why did he have to be so attached to Roy as to feel his death in this way? Why had he become so much more consciously sensitive to the things around him now? Damn his literature at school! It was taking up more of his time than it should do too. Why did his mind keep returning to *Sons and Lovers*? Was it because – ah yes, the deaths in the novel! His elder brother – Paul Morel's elder brother and his mother too – only it was the reverse in his life. His mother first and then his brother after. He wondered whether it was because of his reading of *Sons and Lovers* that he was increasing his own suffering. Could it be that he wanted to feel all that Lawrence's hero felt? Was it because he felt Roy was going to die, that he *would* die? What was it they called it? Telepathy? This transference of thoughts. No that was not possible. Roy could not read his thoughts. Where had he read that a person could will somebody to do something even against that person's will, by an act of concentration? Was such a thing possible? No, he did not want to believe such a thing at all. Was that why Roy had known he had come in the night? Did Roy know that he would not see him again? Roy had said often enough that if he was ever admitted to a hospital he would not leave it alive. What unearthly, supernatural knowledge did Roy have? He had seemed to be getting better. Was it that Roy was willing himself to death? Weren't doctors finding out more and more that the mind was one of the most important factors in the recovery of a patient? Hadn't people lived, by sheer determination, strength of will, when according to material science they should have been dead. Did not the same principal apply to 'Faith Healing', where it was not the miracle of the Lord Jesus Christ or whatever which healed the sick, but the ability of patients to believe themselves cured. Was it not like the man he had read of who could not get an erection with some woman simply because he thought he could not?

He could not go to the hospital. He knew why, but if he told anybody else – no this was not something he could tell anybody, not even Jannet, not now at any rate. Maybe years later, because it would haunt him until he did. How could he go to the hospital expecting and knowing that Roy was dying? There was Jannet! At least he would have the pleasure of contact with her. No, he would not be able to touch her; she would be on duty. That would be painful, just as painful. No, all of these were mere excuses. The fact was, he did not know when – it must have been the previous night – but the conviction, the certainty had come to him that the next time he went to visit Roy, Roy would be dead. He went to the cinema.

Romesh had told him later that night that everybody had asked after him. He did not go on the Saturday either. His

113

father said the same thing to him that night too. It seemed to Dalip that they were accusing him of not caring for Roy. If they knew! If they only knew!

The sun was sharp and stung his face. He parked the cycle. He locked it and looked up. Two of his cousins came down the stairs crying. Dalip knew Roy was dead. He went upstairs, a mere formality. He knew. He went into the room. His father was outside crying. Romesh and some others were also crying. He was alone in the room. The saline bags had been removed, as had the tubes, though the stands were still at the side of the bed. A blanket totally covered Roy or what was left of him. Dalip could not look at Roy. He could not remove the blanket. He was scared. Scared about what he might see, scared that he might cry. He did not want to cry. He would not cry. This was a test, he thought. It sounded nice making resolutions about not being affected by pain or sorrow. He was determined to put into practice the verse from the *Bhagavad Gita* which stated that one should not 'grieve over an inevitable event'. He would not grieve. He felt Roy would have wanted it so. Then he remembered something. Some time ago when they were talking about Madrassis, Roy had said that the Madrassi cried when a child was born and rejoiced when a person died. He had said that when he died he wanted everyone to be happy. Dalip walked out of the room with an expressionless face. He ignored everybody. He walked to the duty room. Jannet was not there. He told the nurse who was there to pass on to Jannet that he had called. He left and went home. He went to bed and slept.

When he woke up there were voices, many voices. He washed his face and went downstairs. There was a tent and many people playing cards and dominoes, or talking in groups. It was eight-thirty. He went upstairs, ate and went downstairs again. His aunts and other women were coming in. He remembered the last time; the pattern was similar. When he went upstairs later in the night the women were talking about how good a person Roy was. All they said was true. Dalip hurried downstairs. Even downstairs everyone who was not playing games or looking on was talking about Roy. Dalip found a worktable away from everybody. He jumped onto it, glad to be alone with his thoughts.

Later his Mamoo joined him. He had been making arrangements with Dalip's father for the cremation. Roy had always wanted to be cremated. Dalip felt guilty, he should have been helping his father with all the arrangements, but he did not feel he could do anything. Then there were so many relatives, young and old. Even the duty of sharing out biscuits and coffee he did not bother himself with, until he saw his cousins doing that task. Just after his Mamoo joined him Romesh joined them. They all sat in silence for some time.

'Today is the thirteenth of June,' Dalip said, 'I will remember this day all my life.' That started the talk, the subject: death. Their Mamoo was a lively man of about twenty-eight; he did most of the talking. He told them of an incident where a man was murdered and that when the murderer appeared at the funeral, the corpse started bleeding from the mouth. He told many serious stories funnily. By and by Dalip started to feel better. Romesh left them. One by one his friends and relatives went home or went upstairs to sleep. Dalip and his Mamoo continued chatting. His Mamoo spoke well of Roy and said he could not remember a wrong that Roy had ever done. It was then that Dalip remembered one, though it was the only one he could think of. His Mamoo remembered it too. One night Roy had come in late. Dalip was reading and it seemed to him that Roy was taking a long time putting away his motorcycle. Dalip went downstairs. The motorcycle was parked under the house but the storeroom door had the key in it as if it had been unlocked. Dalip turned the doorknob and looked in; he was scared that something had happened to Roy. In the dim light of the moon, Dalip saw two naked bodies on the floor. He coughed and walked noisily upstairs. Roy did not have to tell him not to talk.

Roy had told him the girl was a virgin and every afternoon, for about a week, Dalip noted a strange girl passing in

115

the street. One day when Roy, Dalip and their Mamoo were on the bridge the girl passed. She seemed angry and their Mamoo teased her about something. When she had gone out of earshot Roy told them that he'd had sex with the girl in the storeroom on the concrete floor. She'd been a virgin but now he wanted nothing more to do with her. Roy had added that he had not even seen the girl's face properly. They had all started to laugh loudly. The girl turned round. There was hatred in her eyes. She hardly ever walked in the street again.

When they went to bed it was daybreak. Dalip slept until after two o'clock. He bathed and ate. The night passed and so did the next day – Wednesday. Roy would be cremated on the Thursday, very early on Thursday morning. Dalip, his Mamoo and one of his cousins took the wood that would be used in the pyre to the cremation site in a truck. They came home, bathed, shaved, dressed and went back to the cremation site which was some ten miles out of the city. It was their task to see that everything was ready. Dalip was glad he would not be at home when the body was taken there. There would be crying.

Dalip and his Mamoo sat in the shade on the beach and watched the man who would be looking after the burning as he built the pyre. He stacked the lumber neatly, taking his time. It was the first time Dalip had seen a pyre being built. It was the first cremation he would be seeing.

Then the funeral procession arrived. Dalip hardly saw what was happening. He felt he could not bear to look. He stared out to the Atlantic Ocean most of the time. *Bhajans* were sung. The funeral sermon read. The cremation *mantras* read. Then they called him to help light the pyre. He had not seen when it was finished. His back had been turned to them. He alone had not looked. He had been staring at the ocean. The pyre was higher now; Roy was between rows of lumber. Dalip saw the white cotton Roy was on. He did not see the face, he did not want to see the face. He took the lighted stick which somebody gave him and with Romesh lit the pyre. Then he retreated to a rise, standing alone, watching the flames grow, fanned by the wind. The heat was immense. He saw on the other side a familiar figure. In black she looked strange.

The pyre was between them. When the flames went higher she was lost from sight, but reappeared again. Dalip started to smile. He could not say why. He grinned. He felt he would laugh. He had to control his laughter. Death, he thought, look on the tombstone and you will see the name and age of your handiwork; look on the title page and you will see death... death... death... and

> He started laughing
> Uncontrollably
> He flung his hands
> In the air
> He laughed
> Uproariously
> Even when
> He felt
> The hand
> On his arm.

## Epilogue

That hand had finally led him to pieces of his soul he had lost till then, though he had not realised it at the time. Jannet too had helped him find bits of himself – and herself as well. There had been pain, but in the end she had let him go with a generosity which was even graceful. He had had enough of controlled living, controlled love, controlled fun... Didn't Gandhi, the Mahattma, the great soul, exhibit anger and love and sadness, and didn't Gandhi read the *Gita* everyday for decades? And didn't Gandhi commit suicide – knowing there was a gunman and going outside to meet him. But then Gandhi was a realised soul, at least in the days before his death – realised enough to break the cycle of reincarnation.

*Hay Ram* a millisecond before death took a lifetime of effort from the great soul. He had had his share of pain and pleasure before realisation, and so had Sant Valmiki, who had been a highwayman and murderer, and so had Sant Tulsidas, the lover, the husband who gave all, but got heartbreak and grief before he produced the greatest poem in the history of man, the *Tulsi Ramayan*. And Sant Meera and her bhajans... The list was endless and thinking about them Dalip felt the presence of their souls strongly now.

But maybe *The Books* were right. You got married at twenty-five and became a *grihastha*, a householder, until middle age, *then* started the search in earnest. But what if he got sidetracked into so many other things like everybody else – as it was he had to admit that the quest for the flesh had greatly outstripped the quest for the spirit! What if he died before *then* and had to come again.

No! Realisation was better than reincarnation – to become part of the great soul – the *Paramata* – was better than the cycle of rebirths. He had had enough of births and deaths but you could never tell – *Some things you do and some things are done to you!*

The least he could do was try; if death came tomorrow, if death came *now* he could try:

**HAY RAM...**